SAME OLD SHIFT

KILHAVEN POLICE 2

BROCK BLOODWORTH

H. CLAIRE TAYLOR

CONTENTS

CHAPTER ONE_

Officer Norman Green had anticipated many struggles ahead when he signed on as an officer for the Kilhaven Police Department. For one, he was a human working in a metropolis of paranormal beings who were stronger, faster, and sometimes smarter than him. The intelligence thing had nothing to do with them being paranormals, though. Green ran in the middle of the pack when it came to brains. He didn't mind, though; it made it a delightful surprise every time he encountered a too-stupid-to-live opioid-addicted shifter, which generally happened four nights a week.

He also anticipated that one day he might have to take a life when push came to shove. Granted, he hadn't expected it to happen a month out of the academy, and if he'd had to choose, he wouldn't have picked a human to take the bullets, but hell, Green wasn't the one who made the idiot pull a gun on one of his fellow officers.

But one aspect of police work Green hadn't anticipated was the steady flow of gossip within his shift, his sector, and the department at large. The gossip rarely worked in his favor; for instance, it took all of one and a half shifts for the news that he and a particular shriveled taint of a jail nurse had recently split. Because he'd done a commendable job of hiding that he and Nurse Hellstrom were a thing, the news of the split rode high on the wave of the news that they'd been together in the first place. Gossip that rich, covering both the birth and death of a terribly unwise and unprofessional romance, couldn't be contained, and it spread faster than a succubus's herpes.

Occasionally, though, the gossip provided a nice heads up, as was the case when he strolled into show-up the first day after an overtime assignment that had taken a quick turn for the gooey.

While the Kilhaven City Council had yet to approve a budget for the police that would allow for body cameras, there was no shortage of footage of every single police incident in downtown Kilhaven. That reality, much like gossip, could be as much of a blessing as a curse.

For Officer Green and his former field training officer and present nightmarish werewolf shift mate, Officer Heather Valance, it was a temporary blessing. Green could hardly believe what he'd seen with his own eyes—a shifter seizing only a moment before exploding and sending purple goo in every direction, like some fucked up paint grenade. But also, he wasn't sure anyone else would have believed such a thing could happen had it not been caught on multiple cell phones and uploaded through the snail-slow Kilhaven internet to the world wide web.

With cop gossip moving at a quicker pace than the local internet, Green was expecting to see the footage at the shift meeting. Officer Aliyah Brooks had given him the heads up that every shift meeting around the city had the snippet of what had happened downtown cued up to review. So, Green, who'd thus far avoided watching the traumatic—and frankly, mind-boggling—incident was able to mentally prepare himself as he walked into the substation and met with the other Fang 900's at the start of a new week.

Officer Lawrence was the first to notice him enter, and the handsome shifter nodded and said, "How many showers, Green? We have a pool going."

"What?"

"How many showers did you take afterward? I say it was a two-shower night, Harmon says three, and Brooks says four."

Officer Aliyah Brooks, who leaned against the wall between Lawrence and Harmon, scrunched up her face and shook her head slowly. "Four is a low guess. I feel like I might spend an entire weekend soaking in a salt bath, and maybe getting a professional exfoliation after that shit."

"So who was right?" Lawrence prodded.

Green observed his fellow officers as impassively and casually as he could.

Show no weakness.

"Just one."

Harmon and Brooks groaned, but Lawrence just grinned openmouthed and laughed. "That's gross but also pretty stone cold, Green. I've taken two showers for way less bodily fluids. Well done, you sick bastard."

When Officer Valance sauntered in a second later, looking as bored as ever, Brooks hollered, "What about you, Heather? How many showers?"

Valance paused, subjecting her shift mates to her usual dose of bemused scorn, and said, "I don't shower. Where's Sarge?"

"Right here," Montoya said, striding in behind her and taking his place by the projector. He began tinkering with the machine, and by the time he was finished, the rest of the shift had arrived, and he cued up the video, the first blurry frame frozen on the screen.

"I'm sure everyone here has already seen this by now, but we're going to break it down step by step. Valance and Green did a hell of a job, considering. But the department reviewed the footage and has a few additional suggestions to make."

He played the video but hit pause just as it showed Green positioning his thighs under the convulsing shifter's head. "That's exactly what should have been done there. Get a soft part of your body underneath to minimize any potential head trauma, and don't try to restrain the seizing individual, as that can cause unnecessary injury to both parties." He rolled the video again, and as the first splatter of purple found Green's face, everyone in the meeting room groaned, making commiserative gagging noises that did not, in fact, make Green want to gag any less.

Montoya paused the video. "Again, props to Officer Green for remaining calm despite the unfortunate placement of that, um, fluid." Almost as a side note, Sergeant Montoya leaned toward Green and added, "Toxicology still isn't finished, but they did want me to notify you that the sudden ejection of fluids appears to be a reaction to some sort of chemical the deceased came into contact with rather than a result of a viral or bacterial infection. Meaning, of course, it's not contagious."

Green's face heated up. "That's good to hear."

Montoya played the video again, and Lawrence shouted, "Here it comes!" just before Valance got a face full of goo.

Green held his breath and focused on settling his stomach. He shouldn't have eaten so much right before work.

The explosion of the shifter was more appalling this time around than when he'd experienced it firsthand. Viewing it from a distance showed the scope of the blast, and when a small bit of violet dripped down the camera lens and whoever had been filming screamed and ran, the added movement of the camera did nothing to help Green's pulled-pork sandwich stay down.

Montoya cut off the projection. "To recap: in the event that we see another case like this, move underneath the person, using your legs to cushion their head, then wait it out until proper aid can be—"

"All due respect," Valance said. "If I find myself in a similar situation where a man or woman is convulsing on the ground and leaking purple shit, I'm not sticking around to prevent traumatic brain injury. If you look closely,"—she stood, swiped the projector controller from Montoya and rewound the footage until there was a clear shot of her and Green staring down at a pile of purple and bone fragments —"there's no brain left to protect. Or at least not a whole one."

Sergeant Montoya glared at the officer as she shoved the remote back into his grasp. "We don't yet know that this will be the outcome of every subsequent incident of this nature."

"Just saying," Valance replied, "once the goo starts flowing, I'm clearing out. I'd hoped I wouldn't have to mention this, but the night of the incident, I discovered what I concluded to be an *eyelid* lodged between my labia. I'm not joking." She looked around at the other officers who swore and gagged. "I don't understand how it ended up there, either. And trust me, no one wishes more than I do that it hadn't happened, but that's part of my life now. That's a memory I have to live with *forever*."

Sergeant Montoya braced a fist on his hip and pinched the bridge of his nose before looking back up. "The protocol has been established from higher up, Valance. You understood the risks of police work when you got into it, so—"

"Eyelid in the vag? No, Sarge, I did not fully consider the risk of that. But go ahead."

"Jesus Christ," Sergeant Montoya mumbled. "Are you done?"

Officer Valance shrugged a single shoulder, then nodded. "Sure."

———

"Wouldn't be surprised if you get an official commendation, Rookie," Harmon said, leaning against Green's vehicle. Green tried not to look excited by the prospect while he finished loading his gear into the trunk for the night.

"Ain't never seen anything like that," Brooks said, her arms folded across her chest.

"Never seen someone explode?" Green asked off-handedly, attempting to politely continue the conversation without dredging up the visuals anew.

"Nah," said Brooks. "I've seen people explode. Ecuadorians were big on the landmines during the war. Honestly, exploding was one of the better ways to die down there. Boom. Instantaneous. No, I mean the purple. I've never seen anything like *that*."

Green closed the trunk and went around to the passenger's side to throw his large tactical bag onto the floorboard. "Same."

"Really? Never?" Valance said, approaching their triad and including herself in the conversation. "Nothing … oozy and purple?" She stared impatiently at Green who understood, though wished he didn't.

The similarity between the shifter's splatter and the substance that had oozed from puncture wounds on the neck of a deceased human at Shady Grove trailer park just weeks before wasn't lost on Green. That didn't mean he'd officially accepted that the two things were related, though. Accepting such a reality meant opening a door he'd prefer stayed shut; namely, the exit door for this job.

"I think I know where you're going with this," Officer Harmon said, "and I suggest you stop where you are. Just because two substances have the same color doesn't mean they're the same thing."

Valance held up her hands, backing a step off. "You're right. You're totally right. There are so many purple bodily fluids in this world that it would be a stupid conclusion to draw."

Harmon squinted at her resentfully, but Green jumped in before it could escalate. "We should roll out."

"Ooh," Brooks said, scanning him head to boot. "Look who's stepping up and taking charge." She winked at him then, with a smack on his shoulder, made for her car, Harmon following after.

Valance didn't leave for her vehicle yet, though. "You know I have a point."

"I know. Doesn't look like Harmon wants to hear it."

"Well, shit, Rookie. No one *wants* to hear that we might

have a vamp problem on our hands. But you're right. Harmon won't ever come around so long as he's buying what the Church of Dracula is selling. Even when someone inevitably explodes again. And you know it'll happen again, right?"

If the dread roiling in his gut was any indication, he did.

CHAPTER TWO

When the call text came through later that night with "ACTIVE SHOOTER" at the front, Green forgot all about purple goo. He flipped on his lights and sirens, cleared his mind and hoped, from that dark and stifling place near his sternum where this job had forced him to lock away basic survival instinct, that he wasn't the first on scene.

Eden Men's Club had been mentioned more than once in pre-shift meetings. While Green had first assumed it was a strip club, he was informed that it was simply a place for gentleman to get together, enjoy a good shave, smoke a cigar, and swill scotch. Oh, and it was an illegal game room run by a faction of the Greek mob known as the Cherub Mafia.

Occasionally, officers would respond to calls in Eden's parking lot, handling minor disturbances—drunks and druggies fighting, mostly—but orders from the top were to let the operation run unbothered. Then, if all went according to plan, Organized Crime could gather enough intel to either shut the place down for good or pull a drug bust so massive it garnered public favor from the tiny cohort of Kilhaven residents who weren't actively waiting for the drugs to trickle down to them.

But it looked like KPD's hand was being forced on this.

When the call text updated to include, "Suspects: three male leprechauns. Age: unknown," Green nearly veered off the road.

What the hell were leprechauns doing in Fang?

Then he remembered that, technically, Eden was in Ecto sector, which housed a small leprechaun community. The street that ran in front of the notorious game room was the dividing line between sectors. Had the call been anything less urgent, this would have been the Ecto officers' mess to clean.

But an active shooter situation required as much backup as possible, assigned sectors be damned.

Over the handheld, Sergeant Montoya instructed all units in the area to switch to Ecto radio, and Green did just in time to hear Sergeant Pratt from the Ecto 900s order everyone to hold the air.

Officer Frasier, whose reputation as a silent-but-deadly officer had earned him an unpleasant nickname, was the unlucky first on scene. He announced it over the radio and was instructed to hold his position until Corporal Wong arrived to provide backup.

Green turned onto the frontage road near the location and heard the other cars' sirens *en route*. Moments later, Frasier announced three armed suspects were on the run on foot, and he and Corporal Wong were in pursuit.

Over the air came approval from Sergeant Pratt for all able officers arriving on scene to shift at their discretion. It was only the second time in Green's career that he'd been present when such permission was granted sector-wide. The first time had been at a gang fight outside a biker bar, and Green had been left to clean up after the other officers, piling their discarded gear and clothes into his car to play delivery boy once all the action was over.

That call had also ended with Green tasing a suspect in the taint. He hoped this one didn't turn out the same if for no other reason than to avoid the hassle of writing out "frenulum of prepuce of penis" over and over again on another report.

Green swung into the parking lot and jumped out of his car, crouching behind the engine block to scope out the scene. Nothing seemed to be happening. There was a distinct dark blood trail leading away from the building and across the parking lot, sure, but there was currently no movement in view. The suspects that fled on foot and the officers in pursuit were already long gone.

The sound of traffic on the nearby highway felt deafening in the anticlimactic atmosphere. Green was aware of the sirens of other officers drawing closer, but they felt like a hollow gesture, too little too late. Whatever horrific event was destined for this place had probably run its course already. Green could sense that much. But he knew better than to trust his intuition entirely. Doing so was what got officers killed by the more random and desperate acts of violence. Intuition functioned on a set of deeply ingrained assumptions that were built upon the granddaddy assumption of them all: that people would act in specific ways given a specific scenario. Ninety-nine times out of a hundred that might even be a correct assumption.

But in Green's line of work, which put him into contact with more idiotic psychopaths than he cared to admit, that one-hundredth time actually popped up about once or twice a week.

That was where training and protocol came in handy: to eliminate your desire to follow your intuition straight into the nasty end of an assault rifle.

A car whipped into the parking lot. No siren, just a wash of red and blue lights.

Corporal Bannockburn. The werewolf angled his vehicle to block the exit of the parking lot, and jumped out, crouching low as well before motioning at Green and indicating that they should approach the scene now that there were two of them.

The front door of Eden was wide open, but a bright floodlight aimed just beyond the doorstep made it nearly impossible to see inside. A mixture of guttural groans and frantic wailing broke the stillness and spurred Green on, and after pausing for a brief second on one side of the open door, Bannockburn went in first with Green providing cover.

The swanky reception area of Eden was incongruous with the warehouse exterior, but Green didn't have much thought to spare for interior design, considering there were multiple men—were they men? They didn't quite look like men—down. But before he was able to tend to the writhing and moaning cherubim, he needed to help Bannockburn make sure the building was clear of any lingering shooters. The caller had identified three leprechauns, but it could be a deadly mistake to assume any 911 caller in an active shooter situation had a single turd's worth of accurate information. More often than not, it was just one shooter with a semiautomatic who produced the carnage expected of multiple shooters.

And in the case of leprechauns, there was *really* no

telling. As much as Green would never acknowledge it aloud, all those wee folks looked the same to him.

A door that might have otherwise been hidden, flush with the wall and covered in the same obnoxious red and gold fleur-de-lis wallpaper, was dangling on its hinges, leading from the reception room into a back room that was dark by comparison. Heart racing, adrenaline pulsing through his legs, Green clicked on the light at the top of his firearm a moment after Bannockburn did the same. Even if all the leprechauns were gone, there remained the possibility of cherubim opening fire in an attempt to protect their illegal operation.

But everyone who was in that room was either on the floor with an injury, or on the floor crying and begging not to be shot, unaware that this was a new set of men carrying guns, ones that had an easy two feet in height over the last ones.

"Stay down! Don't move!" Bannockburn shouted as he and Green snaked around the slot machines and checked under card tables.

Any one of these people could be a shooter blending in until a chance to strike presented itself. Green's gaze pinballed from one object to the next, his inner monologue shutting down completely to let scattered bits of information move seamlessly through his filter of training and survival instinct.

A puddle of blood stretched out from behind a flashing slot machine with the words *Original Sin* across the front. Bannockburn approached, whipping around the edge, gun out, to find an older woman—shifter of some sort if Green's intense months of scent training were to be trusted— bleeding profusely from the leg, leaning with her back against the wall. She threw her hands up. "Don't shoot! I'm already shot!"

"Hold tight, ma'am," Bannockburn said, nodding to Green, who dropped to his knees, pulling a tourniquet from his belt while dreading the next twenty seconds.

While the corporal provided cover, Green slipped the black strap underneath the gunshot victim's leg and then through the buckle, pulling it until it was snug against her pant leg a few fingers' width above the hole in her thigh. The woman watched silently, sucking in air in sharp bursts. But she wouldn't remain silent for long.

He turned the windlass rod, and after a single rotation, she began cursing, accusing him of trying to cut off her leg. Green struggled to resist the urge to slap his hand over her mouth, instead whispering, "I'm sorry. I know it's painful. I have to do it. Just hold tight. It'll stop hurting in a minute."

Two more turns, then he secured the rod under the clip, finished the job, and stood quickly, biting back the bile rising in his throat.

Bannockburn raised his eyebrows as if to ask, "We good?" and Green nodded, as if to say, "No fucking clue, to be honest, but let's keep going anyway."

They entered a smaller game room where half a dozen people of various species already lay facedown on the floor. A muffled voice shouted, "I work here! I can help!"

Corporal hustled over and lifted the cherub roughly off the ground. "Show us all the rooms."

"They're gone," said the baby-faced man. "They shot up the place and left."

"Show us all the rooms anyway," Bannockburn ordered. The cherub blinked his large round eyes like a were-deer in the headlights, then extended his wings, which poked from two tailored holes in the back of his tailored jacket and had previously been folded out of the way. He fluttered into the air nervously, his arms curled protectively in front of him.

Green followed the manbaby and Bannockburn as they scoured the rest of the building.

"Where else?" Bannockburn asked.

"That's it. That's the whole place."

"Don't bullshit me!"

The cherub flinched. "There's one more."

Green was impressed, but he didn't let it show, at least not to the extent he felt it. He did give his corporal a curt nod of approval just before they entered the final secret room in which the giant safe was kept.

"You happy?" squeaked the cherub. "I'm probably going to get killed anyway for showing you this."

"It'd be weird if I *were* happy in this situation," Bannockburn grumbled before calling clear over the radio. By the time they circled back around to the reception area, more units from Ecto had arrived.

The process of rendering medical aid until the paramedics not only staged but also felt comfortable enough to step out of the safe space of their ambulances to do their jobs, required every officer on scene.

Green's heart continued racing in his chest, making it impossible for him to speak as he knelt down next to an injured cherub man. His knees slipped on the blood-slicked floor as he reached in his vest for the roll of gauze he'd brought with him from his medical bag.

He and Bannockburn had cleared the building, right? So why did he still feel like his life was in imminent danger? Had they missed a room?

"Oh God," moaned the cherub. "I'm gonna die, aren't I?"

"You're not going to die, sir."

The place had hidden rooms. They'd cleared all the ones they knew about, but that didn't necessarily mean—

"No, I'm definitely going to die," groaned the cherub. "I can feel it."

"Please shut up, sir," Green said, unrolling a length of gauze. A bullet had grazed the cherub's side pretty good, and the manbaby was exhibiting signs of shock, so Green allowed him to remain on his back on the ground and shake just a bit while he stared up at the tiled ceiling and whimpered. Though cherubim voices tended to be disconcertingly deep and gravely, that wasn't the case for their agonizing whines, which had an unfortunate childlike quality and echoed like a fallen angel chorus from the wounded around him.

Combined with the baby face and baby body, the infantile cries forced Green to overcome a whole heap of deeply ingrained societal norms before he cut off the bloody shirt and expose the cherub's naked torso. The blood made it difficult to tell the extent of the wound, and once the shirt was off, it looked likely that there might be additional injuries lower on the hip.

With a sigh and a silent reminder that this was a consenting adult and, anyway, it was an extreme circumstance, Officer Green cut away the man's pants as well.

He was fully expecting to find a diaper underneath but was glad when that wasn't the case. Just plain old soiled men's underwear, though probably in a size XXS, which was disturbing in its own special way.

Once a squirt of bottled water had cleared off some the fresh blood, it became apparent that the bullet hadn't so much grazed the man's hip as gone clear through his ... baby fat? Was that baby fat? Either way, the bullet had hit about an inch in and shredded the flesh nearly all the way outward. Only a thin strip of skin held together from below and above, which meant it was time to pack the wound.

God, why? Why couldn't he just die?

Green was pretty sure he didn't mean that.

He grabbed the full roll of gauze from his bag, knowing it would likely take all he had to pack this sucker full. That was the fucked-up part about packing wounds. No matter how minor the bullet hole appeared, no matter what body part it was on, if it was bad enough to require packing, you could count on it being a bottomless pit for gauze.

When he'd practiced it in the academy, his first thought was that they'd hollowed out the entire dummy he was practicing on, that rather than packing the hole in the thigh, he was pushing gauze further and further until it filled up the calf and groin, maybe up into the sternum, even.

Sergeant Jakarta had yelled obscene yet terrifying things at him the whole way: *More, Cadet Green! Pack it harder! Fill him up! Really shove it in there like his life depends on it, because it does!*

In any other scenario, Green wouldn't have been able to suppress a smile at the bounty of double entendres that could be pulled from it, but given the terrifying nature of the sergeant, his mind hadn't gone there until much later.

And then it stayed there. The association between packing a wound and performing rough and debatably consensual sex acts solidified like sediment into limestone, and the first time Green had been forced to do it on the job, he'd felt more like a villain than a hero. He'd hoped that by some stroke of luck, he'd never have to do it again. But he also knew how useless if not cruel hope could be.

The cherub's moans grew fainter as the blood continued to gush.

"Stay awake, sir! I have to pack your wound so it'll stop bleeding. This may hurt."

"Murllllll," gurgled the cherub.

Green grabbed the end of the gauze with his gloved hands and used two fingers to jab it as deep as it could into the cherub's gaping hole.

"Wahhh!" The cherub began wailing in earnest, and the babyish quality could no longer be ignored.

Green grimaced but continued roughly packing the bullet hole. "Hush now, it'll be all right." He jammed more and more in there, the size of the roll already halved.

Just a little more. There's nothing sexual about this. You're saving the man's life. Maybe.

When wet squelching preceded a strong, familiar odor wafting up from the gunshot victim, Green immediately wished the cherub *had* been wearing a diaper when he'd cut off his pants. While bowel evacuation often accompanied death, Green wasn't worried—the cherub continued to whine and moan loudly.

The gauze was already deep red where he'd crammed it in, and when Green was finally sure he couldn't pack anymore, he cut off the remaining strip—all five inches of it —tossed the scrap to the side, and leaned back on his heels to look around.

Those who hadn't been severely injured had already been escorted out, but nearly a dozen cherubim and shifters and a few victims who appeared fully human were being treated by Fang and Ecto officers.

And the whole room smelled like blood and shit.

"I'll go get a medic. Stay here," he said to the cherub he'd just heroically violated before sprinting out of the game room and welcoming the stale Kilhaven air into his lungs.

The parking lot was filled with police cruisers and cops and bloody victims. By the corner of the old building, two plain-clothes detectives listened to an agitated cherub who fluttered in the air at eye level with them as they stood stoically, one listening with his arms folded across his chest, the other taking notes. Green grabbed the medic who looked the least overwhelmed and dragged her behind him toward the reception area. She was young, and as he paused and tried to get a read on her, he couldn't pick up a scent. At least not one *he* could detect, which meant she was human.

I wonder if this is all as weird for her as it is for me?

But then it occurred to him that the smell of feces and guts had lodged itself deep in his nostrils, blocking out the possibility of picking up any less horrific scents, and that she could be anything—human, werewolf, goblin—and his nose wouldn't have told him the difference.

He pulled her out of the bright floodlights of the parking lot and into the dimly lit building.

"There. Bullet went straight through, may have chipped bone. I packed the wound already."

She nodded, taking a deep breath, which seemed an act of bravery in itself while cherubim were shitting themselves left and right, and then swooped in on the victim.

Green slipped outside again.

Bannockburn noticed him almost immediately and hustled over. As he pulled off his soiled gloves, tossing them on the ground for later, he said, "Good work in there, Rookie. You alright?"

"Thank you, sir. Yeah, I'm fine. Gonna need a good shower."

"Or nine." Bannockburn's face softened, a single corner of his mouth curving into a sympathetic frown. "Cherubim shit themselves as a defense mechanism, to invoke a maternal or paternal instinct. They mentioned that in a Little People Intervention class I took probably ten years ago. They'd never teach that in the academy now. Not *PC* to point out." Bannockburn rolled his eyes lightly.

"It didn't work," Green said.

Bannockburn tilted his head back cautiously. "What didn't work?"

"The shitting. I didn't feel paternal."

The corporal chuckled. "No. Me neither."

"So, what now?"

Bannockburn inhaled slowly and fully, hooking his thumbs on his duty belt and letting his shoulders sag as he exhaled. "We keep sticking our hands in blood and excrement until those Organized Crime a-holes tell us we can leave." He nodded over at the plain-clothes detectives.

"I assume we'll be running some people downtown?"

"Psh. Not likely." Corporal shook his head slowly. "Organized Crime will let off all these baby-faced Greek slimeballs. They want the Irish. The Irish are the ones that cause the trouble. Greeks just run their little illegal schemes, make money on the side, buy villas and wives." He ran a palm over his head and blinked away the impending adrenaline crash. "I honestly don't have a clue what might've transpired to get the leprechauns so angry at the cherubim that they'd cause this scene. It'll be a fascinating story to learn." He paused, scanning the parking lot. Those from the Fang 900s who weren't hung up on other calls were assisting. Officer Lawrence was setting out cones to redirect traffic around the entrance to the lot, Marrow had her arms full of water bottles and was distributing them to the victims, and Valance was interviewing a werewolf with a bandage on his head who sat in the back of an ambulance, his legs dangling over the edge.

"Unfortunately," Bannockburn continued, "we'll never hear that story if we leave it up to the Gang Unit. Any witness with half a brain knows not to talk to them. Which is why I gotta talk to some of these witnesses myself."

"Why would they talk to you but not Gangs?"

Bannockburn paused midway through turning to leave. He leaned back slightly, sizing up Green from head to boots. "Valance said you were a good officer."

"Wait, she did?"

"Here's a tip: if you want to be a *great* officer, count to three in your head before asking a question. By the time you finish, you might realize that the question you were considering won't get you the answer you need. After all, ninety percent of what people tell you while you're in that uniform is unpasteurized cow shit. So, sometimes it's better not to ask the question at all and just figure it out yourself."

Not sure how to respond, Green nodded like he understood and said, "Thank you, sir," before wishing he'd said nothing at all.

CHAPTER THREE_

Green was thinking about dead babies as he pulled up to the call address and parked his patrol car a safe distance from the apartment building. Specifically, he was thinking about dead babies with wings and gruff voices, an image that had remained fresh in his mind for two surprisingly slow weeks since the Eden game room shooting.

He read the call text more slowly and paused. Huh. He'd missed that detail the first time through. Pressing the *Dispatch* button on his Human Accessible Monitor, he spoke directly to the call taker for clarification. "Fang 9-07 on scene at Polk Boulevard. Am I reading the call text right? Is that supposed to say Latin?" he asked.

He recognized Ricky's voice immediately as it piped out of a speaker. "Yes. The caller specified that it sounded like Latin."

"The caller can recognize Latin?"

"Beats me. She just said it 'sounds like Latin' not that it necessarily *was* Latin."

"Okay, thanks, Ricky."

Well, shit. While his family had been staunchly religious growing up—he suspected more as a weapon to constantly punish Keller and Kim and him for being human than for any spiritual reason—he hadn't been the kind of religious that knew much about Latin.

So, his mind immediately went to the only trivia he knew about the language, all of which he'd learned from the police academy slide about demons. It had included a bulleted list of the common signs of demonic possession. He tried to remember them all, but the one that was leaping off the projector screen of his mind was, *Speaking a language that sounds like Latin.* Considering he wouldn't know Latin from Italian from Hobgoblin, he was thankful that the caller had mentioned the red flag.

Once *sounds like Latin* had stopped demanding his mental attention, the remaining signs of demonic possession were allowed to surface. Smell of sulfur. Dilated pupils. Dead stare. Walking on walls/ceilings. Murdering loved ones. Taunting cops with villainous clichés like, "You think *you* can stop *me?*"

Green parked a house down from the address and popped the trunk. Remembering with a twinge of shame his first drastically botched poltergeist call, he was determined to arrive better prepared for spiritual warfare. He'd fielded a couple minor ghost calls since, but this was his first demon. Ever. And the last thing his increasingly tolerable reputation needed was for SHU to have to swoop in and exorcise *him.* Assuming he'd survive it, he would still have to face the rest of his shift at show-up the next day, and he might not live through that kind of humiliation.

How much of his career was dictated by a desire to avoid humiliation, he wondered.

Doesn't matter. Focus. Get your head on straight, Rookie.

Following the slide about signs of demonic possession was one titled *Preparing for a demonic encounter.* What were the bullet points on that one? There was *Bring holy water.* He checked the vial on his belt. It was full, but he grabbed a backup anyway, slipping it into his pants pocket. *Ward yourself* was the next helpful hint. Except he forgot how to do it. Something with salt maybe? It was usually salt.

He opened up the bulky supply bag that he almost never touched, pulled out a salt shaker, sprinkling a few grains into the palm of his hand before rubbing his hands together and then slapping himself on the cheeks a few times. That should do.

Then he pulled out a small bundle of sage and a lighter, waiting for the sage to catch, stoking it, then blowing it out and drawing small circles around himself for protection.

He stared down at the smoking sage, waiting for the smoldering embers to die. This was taking too long.

Tossing the sage onto the street and stomping it with his boot, he hoped he wasn't unintentionally cursing himself. There was no logic with this magic stuff, so it was anybody's guess what small shortcut or modification might accidentally doom a person to damnation or whatnot.

He stared down at the smushed sage bundle, where it continued to smoke despite his haphazard effort to extinguish it. "Shit." He picked it up and sprinkled a little holy water on the burned end. There. Good enough.

Tip number three was *Show no fear.*

He slammed the trunk shut, remembered tip number four, *Read the passage,* and immediately opened the trunk again, grabbing the laminated slip of paper with the necessary passage on it and jamming it into his breast pocket next to his notepad.

Okay. All good, and ready to rock and roll. Or I'm fucked. One or the other.

Without his red and blue lights, which he'd decided against to allow himself the element of surprise (and, technically, it was just a check-welfare call, so it wasn't required) the parking lot was dark as he crossed through, making for building 13. While that building number seemed a little too on the nose, he supposed that if he responded to enough demon possessions, one was bound to be in a building 13.

He climbed a flight of stairs and paused outside the door of the apartment, leaning close and listening for anything that sounded like Latin, which for him included anything that wasn't English.

What he heard was something like Spanglish, which only served to complicate the matter and convince Green that one of two equally likely scenarios awaited him beyond the flimsy front door, though he couldn't be sure which: a demonic possession or an English speaker reading off a Mexican food menu very loudly.

He hoped for the latter, but prepared himself for the former, banging on the door. "Kilhaven Police."

The response was a maniacal bray.

God dammit.

"Police! Open the door!"

Officer Green jumped back, shuffling to the side of the frame when the door whipped open, the handle crashing into the interior wall. A gust blew out that smelled like a giant boiled egg had just shit out a pile of smaller boiled eggs, and Green resigned himself to the fact that he was now face-to-face with legitimate demonic possession. He waited, holy water in one hand, gun in the other, but nothing moved, nothing made a sound. With a deep breath to steady himself, Green peeked around the door frame and into the apartment. Against the far wall of the gloomy living room stood a pale-skinned man in nothing but off-white briefs staring at Green through the gloom. His dead-eyed stare widened, and he cackled.

Green radioed in a confirmed possession, requesting backup.

"Sir, is there anyone else in the apartment?" Green asked, keeping his distance and following protocol as best he could. His goal here wasn't to exorcise the man—SHU would be on scene shortly to handle that—but to make sure there was no one else at risk while the possession continued. He'd heard that demons liked to put on a show, and it was rare that a possession would take place with no one else around to witness it, though it wasn't entirely unheard of. Officer Harmon claimed he'd once caught a possessed woman watching soap operas from her ceiling with no one but a few terrified cats to bear witness.

The possessed man didn't respond, instead darting down a hall and out of sight.

Green shut his eyes for a second, cursing his luck. Without knowing whether or not someone else could be held hostage in the apartment, he would have to pursue and hope backup arrived shortly. He stuffed the holy water back into its holster and put both hands on his gun. Shooting a possession victim wasn't ideal, but it was better than being killed by one.

He tiptoed across the carpeted living room, zigzagging to avoid the toppled furniture as he approached the open door at the end of the hallway, from which white-blue glowed. Since he hadn't heard the demon shutting a door and couldn't imagine one doing it quietly, the first room to clear was that one.

Listening intently for signs of anyone besides the demon, Green suspected he was being led into a trap, but his job required him to walk straight into it and trust that his training would serve him to find his way out again.

When the floor creaked beneath his left boot, he froze. But nothing jumped out at him. The apartment was still silent as death, including the room at the end of the hall. Fifteen feet remaining, he swallowed down the adrenaline.

A hand grabbed his shoulder just before he entered the short hallway, and he whirled around, ready to unload into whoever had managed to sneak up on him so stealthily.

Officer Valance's icy blue eyes met his, and she shoved the barrel of his gun toward the floor with a flat palm, whispering, "Stop being an idiot." In her other hand, she held a brightly colored parody of a machine gun, which she pointed toward the ceiling.

Green stared at it, unsure what to make of it. "Is that police issued?" he whispered.

"Dumb questions later." She stepped in front of him, holding the water gun out in front of her as she pumped it to maintain the pressure. Before he followed, he swapped out his gun for a vial of holy water, feeling quite literally outgunned by his former FTO.

She paused before the open door and glanced back, catching Green's eyes. She motioned to her own, mouthed, "Look" then mimicked running with her fingers and mouthed, "Run."

Green understood. As soon as they were sure no one else was in harm's way, it was time to clear the fuck out.

Valance made her move, and Green was right on her heels.

The scene in the bedroom wasn't pretty. The space was in the middle of being ransacked, as if someone had pressed a pause button, with clothes and wall decorations strewn around and others hovering in midair.

While tighty-whitey floated a few inches off the ground himself, cackling pointlessly as his eyes locked onto Valance, a naked woman moaned on an exposed mattress in the far corner.

"She's yours, Green. I got this asshole." She pumped her water gun.

Said asshole laughed, except the voice was now low and deep like a black pit. The demon shouted, "You think *you* can stop *me?* I was devouring souls eons before the first mangy werewolf set paw on this earth. I've conquered more — Aw shit! Ahhh!"

Valance unloaded the holy water in a shockingly high-powered stream, keeping her finger on the trigger as she pumped and pumped and pumped to maintain the pressure.

She wouldn't manage it much longer, though. That tank had to run out sometime.

Green sprinted over to the woman and dumped the vial of holy water on her. When it didn't cause any noticeable effect, other than making her exposed skin a little wetter and washing away some of the blood from cuts on her ribs, he grabbed her, flung her over his shoulder, and ran like hell, trying not to hit any part of her on the door frame or walls, though, admittedly, it wasn't the end of the world if he did, so long as he managed to get both of them out of there alive.

She groaned as he took the stairs quickly and felt her stomach and the bottom of her ribcage smash against his shoulder with each hurried step. No time to adjust. He didn't stop running until he was all the way across the parking lot by building seven. Only then did he lay the woman down on the grass and have a thought to spare for her possibly cracked ribs. She moaned and rolled around a little, and as he turned to get eyes on Valance, he spotted the officer hurriedly backing out of the front door, the last of her holy water running dry.

"Fuck!" she shouted, her voice echoing through the complex. Then she started hollering something else as she sprinted away. Words Green didn't understand.

"Oh. Right." He reached in his breast pocket, touching the laminated card with the passage in Latin. It occurred to him that he should spend his next weekend memorizing the verses like Valance had, though even as he thought it he understood that he would probably spend the following weekend the same way he spent every weekend: drinking, sleeping, and switching between action movies and pornography.

He'd never seen Valance run away from something like that before, shouting and yelling, wouldn't have thought it a possibility before then. That didn't bode well for anyone. SHU had their work cut out for them whenever they arrived.

"Turns out that bastard is a shifter," she said, skidding to a halt next to Green, and quickly turning to face the apartment again. She rolled her shoulders back, straightening in a futile attempt to regain composure, then glanced toward Green. "I dunno if you've ever had a goat charge you, but that's nothing to play around with. They line up their spine." She held out her arm, making a fist and punching the air with it. When Green didn't respond right away, she lowered her hand. "Doesn't matter. Is she all right?" She nodded toward the moaning woman, who Green had mostly forgotten about.

"Oh shoot. Um." He knelt down next to her. "Ma'am, can you speak at all?"

She moaned.

"I mean, besides that," Green clarified. "Can you speak words?"

"You throw holy water on her?" Valance asked.

"Of course."

Valance dangled her spent water gun over the woman anyway, flinging the last few drops onto her. When nothing happened, she seemed satisfied and jogged over to her vehicle for her first aid bag.

By the time SHU arrived a few minutes later, Valance and Green had washed the woman's wounds, which were mostly superficial and likely inflicted for purposes of blood ritual rather than as an attempt to genuinely injure her. They'd also wrapped her in a blanket, for modesty's sake more than to keep her warm; the perpetually humid, stagnant air was sufficient for that.

Agents Saffron, Stonewall, and a new hag Green hadn't met before jumped out of the SHU van, readying to go in. Agent Saffron paused when she reached Valance and Green. "She clean?" She nodded at the woman on the ground.

"All good on her. The demon is super pissed, though. And a shifter."

Agent Saffron didn't seem concerned, or perhaps her game face was just that good. "Goat?"

"Yep. Big ol' thing."

She joined the other two agents, and the three charged forward as quickly as their stubby legs and round bodies allowed, each with a large, bulging leather pouch slung over a shoulder.

"Should one of us provide backup?" Green asked.

Valance scoffed. "Hell no. They have hundreds of years of experience between them. We'd only get in the way. You especially."

The woman wailed from the curb beside them. "Don't let them hurt Curtis!"

Valance's head swiveled around. "Oh, you talk now? Great. What's Curtis's last name?"

The corner of the woman's top lip cinching up toward her nostrils. "Buckhammer maybe?"

Green tried not to groan his impatience. Until this job, he'd always assumed every adult knew the last name of the person they lived with, not to mention the one they claimed they were in love with.

Add that to his long list of busted assumptions about the basic functionality of adults.

"Date of birth?" Valance asked pleasantly.

"Um ..." The woman shut her eyes, shaking her head minutely. If she didn't know the guy's last name, it would make sense that she didn't know when he was born. Unfortunately, it made looking him up in the database just about impossible. But then she produced one, and Valance turned to Green. "Go run that. I'm gonna take her to the hospital."

Green did as he was told, only vaguely aware that he was still following Valance's commands even though he no longer had to. After a few fruitless attempts with the name

Curtis Buckhammer, he entered the date of birth again, then typed the name slower to let autofill work its magic. B-U-C—

The name Curtis Buchanan popped up, and Green wasn't especially shocked by what appeared in the records.

But it did mean he would have to stick around a while longer.

He knocked on the driver's window of Valance's car, and she rolled it down. "Multiple felony warrants for distribution of meth and practicing of illegal magic."

"You got him then?" she asked.

"Yeah, I'll stick around."

When a blinding orange light flashed behind the closed blinds of the apartment, Green had to remind himself that the hags had it covered and he didn't need to intervene. It was difficult, but conjuring up the image of the possessed man and the look on Valance's face as she sprinted down the stairs was enough to quell any urge to go be a hero.

And before long, Agent Saffron emerged from the front door a step behind the man, who was still in his underwear but was now also wearing a shiny set of silver handcuffs. The other agent Green didn't know followed closely after, but Stonewall remained inside, closing whatever doorway had been opened.

Thick blood dripped from multiple cuts on Curtis Buchanan's chest, the placement of the incisions mimicking those found on the victim. Green was absolutely sure those weren't there before SHU ran inside, but he decided not to ask questions. The hospital could handle that. Also, questioning hags fresh off a good spell session was inadvisable. The invisible aura of power still fluttered around them like steam radiating off an athlete's shaved head after a winter workout.

"Officer Green?" croaked the SHU agent he didn't know.

"Yes, ma'am."

She didn't proffer a hand as she stopped short of him, and that was fine by Green. He didn't particularly want to touch her. She looked like she was wearing a mask of a fairly attractive woman in her fifties, not too unlike one he'd left a bar with a few weekends back. Except he would never consider taking this one back to his place, because even as his eyes told him one thing, his mind was certain that behind that mask was some sort of decay. And odds were against the hag having taken the same care with her body below the SHU cloak as she did with her face.

Her smokey eyes bore into him. "He'll need to go to the hospital. Obviously, we're not allowed on the premises, so it's on you."

"Yes, Agent …"

"Cork."

"Agent Cork. Not a problem. That's why I stuck around." He glanced over her shoulder at where Curtis, guarded by Agent Saffron, sat on the bumper of the SHU van in a daze. And when Green looked back to Agent Cork, she was still staring at him unblinkingly.

"You want me to clear your energy? It's looking a little dark now. You have quite a few soul pieces stuck to you."

He shook his head a single time. "Nope. I'm good. Thank you, though." He grinned, and it wasn't returned. Instead, the gray of her irises fogged slightly, and the corners of her mouth went slack as her lips parted.

"Careful out there, Norman. Humans are missing, being killed in droves."

He took a quick half step back. "Huh? I haven't heard anything about that. What are you—"

She blinked quickly and her irises cleared. "Oh, sorry. No, of course you haven't heard anything about it. It hasn't happened yet." She chuckled, or at least that was what he assumed the noise indicated, though it sounded more like someone shaking a bag of dry rice. "Sometimes I get a little mixed up about future and past." She leaned forward, and her breath smelled like the old potpourri his grandmother used to stuff in his underwear drawer when he'd visit her in the summer. "Don't mention it to IA, yeah?"

"Of course not."

Agent Saffron approached with Curtis by her side, still in cuffs. Strands of her silver hair had shaken loose from her hood during the fray. "He's all clear, but as you can see, we had to cut him." She grinned sheepishly, showing off a mouthful of too many teeth.

Agent Cork nodded supportively. "Sometimes you just have to cut them." She turned to Green. "Okay, all yours, Rookie." The hags handed off the suspect and left Green to wonder what in the hell Agent Cork was talking about. Not the cutting. The other bit. Humans dying in droves? That couldn't be good.

Welp, there was no point in worrying about the details, he supposed.

Whenever it started happening, odds were high that his unlucky ass would be the first on scene to learn more.

CHAPTER FOUR

Jail used to be a welcome break for Green. It was an oasis of safety compared to the streets of Fang. While he was out on said streets, his hypervigilance ratcheted up immediately, and he didn't notice the heightened state and how much energy it required to exist like that. But as soon as he stepped through the doors leading into Shankwright County Jail, the stress dissolved, like touching base in a game of tag.

Sure, jail bragged a higher density of felons than a mucker family reunion, but it also contained a higher density of cops, many of whom had started to treat Green with something not entirely like disdain. Was it respect? A boy could dream.

But that sense of relief upon entering into the inexplicably moist air conditioning was gone now because the jail was where Nurse Hellstrom was more nights than not. It'd always been where he could expect to see her, typing notes behind the intake desk or calmly leading a rowdy patient to a private examination room, but the significance of her presence had done a one-eighty in his life recently.

As he led Curtis Buchanan toward the desk after a long bit of bonding time at the hospital where the suspect had shown little remorse over the part he played in inviting a demon to inhabit his body, Becky Hellstrom was the first to spot them enter, and she smiled.

"Officer Green," Hellstrom said politely like they hadn't humped like hares in springtime for two solid months.

"Nurse," he said, keeping his voice low in an attempt at composure and dominance. It was something he'd noticed Valance do before, and it'd always worked for her. Or maybe she just *was* composed and dominant, and the voice thing had little to do with it. "Just got Mr. Buchanan through Kilhaven Memorial, so we're heading straight to booking."

She chewed her bottom lip, feigning concern. "I don't know. I think I should check him out. What are the charges?"

He sighed but decided to play along. "Dark magic. Demon possession."

"Ah, I see." She frowned apologetically. "Have you done a cavity search?"

"Have I—What? No, you know that's against policy."

Her eyes lingered on Curtis just a little longer than was polite. "Yeah, well, sometimes they hide hex bags in their anus. If the hospital didn't complete one, then I must."

"I ain't got nothing up my asshole!" Curtis protested.

"We'll see about that. Sign this." Becky slid a clipboard across the desk, and Green groaned, unlocked the handcuffs so Curtis could sign the consent form, and then waited as the man read it over.

He looked up from the form to stare at the nurse. "So, you don't put your finger in my butthole?"

"No, sir. I just look into your mind."

"What's the fun in that?"

Green shoved Curtis. "Just sign the damn form, or I'll get Nurse Ulster to do the search, and trust me, she's not exactly gentle. You thought those cuts on your chest were bleeding heavily, just wait."

Curtis leered at Green but signed the consent form all the same.

"Perfect," Becky said. "Now shut your eyes, Mr. Buchanan."

He did, and Green clicked the handcuffs back on him.

"Hot damn!" Curtis shouted after a short pause, his eyes shooting open. He twisted around to stare at Green with something akin to adoration. "I didn't know a man could bend like that."

"Huh?" Then it clicked.

Green smacked the desk and leaned over it, hissing, "Don't you *dare*, Hellstrom. I didn't do anything to you. *You're* the one who screwed *me* over."

Becky kept an innocent smile on her lips, and Curtis jumped in with, "I'd say you were both screwing each—"

Green rounded on him. "Right to remain silent, Curtis!"

Becky sighed, switching precisely from an innocent smile to hurt puppy dog eyes. "I don't know why you're upset or what you think I did, but I didn't do anything. I just did a cavity search, as authorized by this form."

Green clenched and unclenched his jaw. Yelling at her would do no good and could lose him his job. It wasn't worth it. "Who else have you shown?" he muttered.

She paused, and he could see the wheels turning behind her eyes. "No one," she finally said.

Green leaned closer. "You swear?"

Her shoulders softened, and she looked away for a moment, exhaling before meeting his eyes again. "Yes, Norman. I swear. I shouldn't have lashed out at you. You're completely right. I'm sorry."

That tone. That gentleness. It was the Becky he'd gotten to know so well in his bed. God, how he missed it.

"I will violently vomit three days' worth of food"—his nostalgia was interrupted by a woman's deep voice from the direction of the break room—"if I'm subjected to *one more* mental frame of this amateur porno!"

Officer Valance charged over to the intake desk, nearly knocking an Imp sector officer's feet out from under him. The bright blue of her eyes, which were locked onto Becky Hellstrom, transitioned to amber, a helpful little warning sign built into werewolves' biology.

"Oh right," Becky said to Green, "and I might have shown your new girlfriend." She shot him a sarcastic smile.

Green scrunched up his face. His new girlfriend? There was that woman at the bar, but he'd hardly call her his girlfriend. "What are you—Wait, Valance? You think I'm dating Valance?"

Before he could get an answer, Officer Valance swooped down on the nurse, who was forced to lean back in her rolling chair to avoid a face full of Valance's face.

"Listen here, you shriveled taint. Not a second more of that. I don't want to see a single second more of you two writhing like awkward teens on a soiled mattress. Not only will I make sure that every drop of my vomit lands on something you love that cannot be replaced, but I will personally make sure you don't set foot in this jail again, except in the case that you're arrested for being a heinous bi—"

"Valance," Green said hurriedly. While he did enjoy seeing Hellstrom sweat, Valance was about to cross a line. Assuming she hadn't already with the "shriveled taint" comment.

Valance snapped her jaw shut but continued to glare at Nurse Hellstrom. "Do we have an understanding?"

Becky said nothing, but Valance straightened up, scoffing. "Good. And go ahead, call me whatever you want. You think I haven't heard worse? I've heard worse in multiple languages. You should hear the terms they come up with in South America."

Oh damn, she was mentioning South America already? Definitely time to wrap up the show before the PTSD came out full force.

"Officer Valance, will you help me get Mr. Buchanan through booking?" Green asked, trying to pull the plug on this whole ugly encounter.

Valance scrunched up her nose at him like he'd just farted sulfur. "You still need me to hold your hand? Jesus. Can't anyone just do their damn job around here?" She stomped away, ending the encounter, and Green, careful not to accidentally catch the eye of his former lover turned pain in the ass, shoved Curtis just a little too hard toward the hallway leading back to booking.

Curtis grunted. "I thought *I* had bitch problems. But, boy, you got some serious shit going on."

CHAPTER FIVE_

When the call came out the following night for all units in the area to head directly to Feeney's Shillelagh, Green assumed it was regarding some sort of revenge hit from the cherubim mafia.

Feeney's was the only leprechaun bar in Kilhaven. It was just a few miles down the road from the game room at Eden Men's Club and also nestled on the border of Ecto and Fang. Green wasn't sure if the sector borders had been drawn like they were to allow the department to pull from two sectors as needed to maintain peace between groups that had a long and bitter history, or if both the leprechauns and cherubim had intentionally set up shop along the established sector line because they knew that, in practice as opposed to theory, things were generally more disorganized when cops from different sectors, functioning on different radio channels, had to coordinate. That kind of confusion had certainly worked in criminals' favor before.

When Green arrived on scene, there were no fluttering wings and baby faces to be found. But there didn't need to be; the leprechauns could start a disturbance all on their own, and a massive brawl was in progress, despite Corporal Singh shouting through a bullhorn from a safe distance.

Two leprechaun-related calls in just under a month was unusual. Green certainly hadn't seen it in his short time on the Force. Not to say leprechauns didn't get into trouble, because they did. But they were almost impossible to catch *causing* the trouble. God only knew how many unresolved incidents were perpetrated by those tiny men and women before they fled the scene undetected. They were a slippery bunch, and catching them in the act was a rarity.

But it was starting to look like the Irish were getting sloppy.

"Steer clear," Corporal Singh warned Green as he approached. "The fighting sticks are a-flying! Take one of those in the back of the head, and next thing you know, you'll be waking up in the hospital with the worst luck you've ever experienced. Best to just sit back and let the little guys wear themselves out."

"Whatever you say, sir." Green waited with Corporal and a few other officers from the Ecto 700s. But as time passed, none of the leprechauns seemed to tire. "You sure we shouldn't just pepper spray them? What if one of them gets killed?"

Singh arched a judgmental eyebrow at Green. "You want to pepper spray a bunch of leprechauns? Be my guest. *If* one of them doesn't curse you, you'll still have same elven media to answer to. They'll eat that story right up. It'll be all over the news." He chuckled to himself and shook his head. "Nah, the public has a soft spot for leprechauns. The elves especially. They got the whole immigrant plight thing going for them. Everyone loves an underdog."

The crack of shillelagh against bone echoed from the center of the fighting ring.

"I don't know about the whole underdog thing," Green said. "Those guys can fight."

They did eventually tire themselves out, though, or at least the fighting became so sloppy that the audience tired and crept away, casting nonchalant glances at the police presence. Without an audience, those fighting in the center lost either interest or their adrenaline rush, and by the time only a dozen people were left in the parking lot, too drunk or high to realize it was in their best interest to split, Green and the rest of the officers moved in to begin detaining those involved in the brawl.

As Green struggled to perform the sobriety test on an intoxicated subject with a large knot rising up from just below his hairline, he suppressed a growing impatience. Firstly, getting a leprechaun to look you in the eye was tricky enough in a casual encounter where alcohol and authority didn't come into play. There was also the let-down making him a little cranky. This was a call that could have easily spiraled out of control but instead turned out to be relatively uneventful. It was nearly impossible to tell how a call would pan out. The ones that seemed the most urgent often de-escalated quickly without much effort on the part of law enforcement, while the ones that seemed routine could become a three-ring shitshow without a moment's warning.

The fight at Feeney's fell into the better of the two categories, so Green decided not to let it get to him that eye tests were futile, meaning he would have to fall back on other charges of disorderly conduct and assault for the arrest.

As Green shut the back door of his cruiser, where his suspect was passed out on his side on the backseat, and opened the driver's side door, Delmar from the E700s shouted, "Suspect down!" and instinctively Green knew this call had just pulled another about-face.

He rushed over to where one of the leprechauns who'd taken the worst beating flopped like a fish on the parking lot asphalt. Officer Delmar's reaction was pitiful; he knelt next to the body, using his hands as padding for the man's head, which, of course, did about jack squat. Delmar grimaced each time the leprechaun's skull crushed his knuckles against the hard, textured ground, and without a second thought, Green shoved the officer aside, allowing him to slip his thighs underneath the man's bruised and swollen head.

"Must be a concussion or something," Delmar said, scrambling to his feet while staring down at the tiny thrashing body.

It was possible, Green supposed. Swelling of the brain could cause something like this, but deep in his gut, he already knew that wasn't what was happening here.

When the first bit of purple oozed from the leprechaun's nose, Green gritted his teeth against the impending mess.

"Get me a rain poncho," he barked at Delmar or any of the other half-dozen officers just standing around. He didn't give a rat's ass who did it, so long as it happened. Immediately.

Corporal Singh bent down, slightly out of breath, and stuck a thick gag in the leprechaun's mouth to keep him from swallowing his own tongue or biting it off.

But Green knew any effort to save the man's tongue would soon be wasted.

"Poncho!" Green yelled at the corporal before he could

catch himself. The first trickle of purple flung free from the leprechaun's ear, hitting Green's uniform just below the top button. "Poncho! Poncho! Poncho!" He couldn't tell if it were his frantic screaming or the increase of flung goop that caused the other officers to jump back. It didn't matter.

Because, in the end, the leprechaun still exploded in a burst of gold sparkles and violet fluids.

And Green still found himself covered head to boot in flesh and slime.

And fragments of the deceased's skull still rested on Green's bruised thighs.

"God"—mucusy purple dripped from his eyebrow, landing on his chin—"dammit." He stared down at the mess as strings of it slumped like rope bridges between his outstretched legs. Then he leaned to the side on one elbow and threw up the tuna fish sandwich he'd eaten in his car a few hours before.

While the pile of warm, moderately digested canned fish was unpleasant, it didn't look or smell out of place with the new aesthetic of the parking lot.

The other officers, who were relatively unscathed, scurried around frantically. Singh, a man known for his composure after having re-upped with special forces in the thickest part of the South American conflict, shouted at his handheld radio like it was responsible for what had just happened before his very eyes.

As two officers in gloves lifted him off the ground, and he both felt and heard the thick clumps of Irishman slip off him and splat onto the parking lot, one clear thought permeated the fog.

I should probably talk to Valance about this.

CHAPTER SIX

Two days later, Sergeant Montoya stood to the left of the projector screen and pointed at the horrifying tableau, at the center of which sat Green, his legs outstretched, his navy blue uniform already taking on splotches of purple. If he never saw that scene again, it would be too soon.

The still image had been pulled from one of the dash cams, pre-explosion, yet the violet was visible even over the distance of approximately twenty feet between the crisis and the camera.

Montoya gestured to the screen. "Update to the protocol. Green." The sergeant pointed at him, and Green could feel the rest of the shift's attention move his way. "You did the right thing. Again. Great work."

Green didn't bother smiling but nodded once.

"And the rest of you, here's the update. Rather than standing around with your thumbs up your bums, one of you will shout 'poncho' in response, and that means you've assumed responsibility for bringing the man on the ground a rain poncho, asap. You will sprint to the closest one available to you and sprint back—I repeat, *sprint*—unfolding it along the way so that you may assist the officer on the ground in putting it on. Then you will move back twenty feet to avoid the blast radius along with every other non-poncho-ed officer in the vicinity. You have Green to thank for this clever idea, as he was the first on scene to mention a poncho." He nodded more approval at the rookie.

"Just so we're clear," Officer Tara Marrow said, "we're not doing anything to *stop* the explosion? Just to protect ourselves from it?"

Montoya bristled. "For now, yes. Forensics and the medical examiner's office are working around the clock to figure out what is happening, so until they do, our only recourse is to protect our officers and the safety of the public." He paused, sucking in air through his large, bullish nostrils. "Any other questions?"

Green suspected that there were too many rather than none, but Montoya seemed fine with the silence anyway.

"Okay, next up. Day shift has been looking for a missing Crown Tree girl. Name Anna Marie Pfaff. Age ten. Father is a telepath, mother is a human, and as far as they know, Anna is a human as well." He flashed to the next slide, and a class picture appeared on the screen. "But as you can tell from the baby face, she hasn't hit puberty, so there's always a chance that she's telepath or, hell, anything, really. You know how rich women can be when their husbands aren't around. We've each seen it a million times.

"Anyway, the girl went out to recess yesterday and never made it back in. No one saw where she went." He flipped to another image of her, this one with her arm slung around an even tinier girl who looked remarkably like her. "Anna is one of four. She has an older brother who, turns out, is a werewolf—we'll leave the conclusions to geneticists on that —and an older sister who is perfectly human. Then she's got the little sister pictured here.

"Mrs. Pfaff comes from werewolf parents, so either she was carrying on a long affair with a werewolf, or the recessive gene is being passed along, first to the son and possibly to the daughter. This has all the signs of a first-shift runaway."

"Did the parents mention whether the daughter had friends at school?" Valance asked from the back of the room.

Montoya stared at her suspiciously. As he probably should, Green supposed, considering Valance only ever spoke during show-up when she had something to say that might make Montoya look unprepared or blustering. "Parents say she had a lot of friends, which is why it's so strange that she would take off if it weren't for something sudden like sprouting hair on her hands or growing a tail."

"So," Valance continued, "you're saying she has a lot of friends, was out at recess, where friends are notorious for spending time together, and none of them reported seeing her shift?"

Montoya shrugged it off. "Maybe they were playing hide and seek, and she shifted while she was hiding."

Valance chuckled dryly. "Oh boy, that's some great police work, Sarge. 'She was probably playing hide and seek at the exact moment she shifted for the first time.' You said she has an older sister. Do we know when *she* hit puberty? Generally, siblings of the same sex don't have too much of a discrepancy."

Montoya grunted. "I don't know if the officers on scene asked about her sister's first menses, no. What are you on about, Officer?"

Valance stepped back, leaning against the far wall again as she held up her hands in mock surrender. "Nothing, Sarge. Just that, well, you know, sometimes we have a rash of missing children, the cases end up closed, but it's never publicized what happened. Were the children found dead? Did they return home?" She bared her teeth in what Green presumed was intended to be a smile. "Remember the last time?"

Montoya narrowed his eyes, and for a moment, he seemed to be considering her words. Then he said, "Do you need to take some mental health days, Valance? I haven't a goddamn clue what you're getting at, and frankly, we don't have time for it." He aimed his eyes at the fiberboard ceiling tiles, refocused, and flipped to the next slide, which continued the BOLOs for the day. Green tried to catch Valance's eye, but she was too busy sharing a knowing look with Corporal Bannockburn, who seemed much less dubious of her suspicions than the sergeant. His arms were crossed over his chest as he nodded minutely at her then returned his attention to the front.

And while Green couldn't yet assemble a coherent theory, he felt in his gut that he and Valance were collecting pieces of the same puzzle. But whatever it was, there was a reason she wouldn't come out and say it, and if Valance was hesitant to bring it up, Green best keep his damn mouth shut about it until something more obvious surfaced.

———

Green yawned as he leaned against his car just after midnight, staring across the frontage road to the interstate. Cars zoomed by, the drivers likely curious about the cause for the multiple police vehicles with lights flashing but otherwise unaware of the dead body lying in the grass.

Having arrived fourth to the scene, his job was simple: park his car, make sure no drunks or transients or drunk transients wandered over to see what was up. Brooks had been the first on scene after the body was reported, and while that normally wouldn't matter and the responsibility of writing up the report would fall to Green since he was the rookie, Bannockburn had made sure that wasn't the case for this particular call.

The vic was a cherub, and after the game room incident and the exploding leprechaun, it was clear something was up between the two groups. Detectives from Organized Crime had been called in, and Bannockburn insisted a seasoned veteran write up the report to make sure rules were followed to the letter and this evidence couldn't be thrown out in court. While it was a bit of a blow to Green's ego, his disappointment didn't linger. For one, he'd never been a strong writer, and his reports left something to be desired; namely, the logical order of information. But mostly, it meant he wouldn't be stuck on this call all night and wouldn't have to look at the dead baby in the grass, whose wings had been hacked off, hopefully post-mortem, any longer than he had to.

Green watched another very possibly drunk driver slam on his brakes on the interstate upon noticing the police presence, swerving slightly before speeding off. Bannockburn appeared next to Green.

"Organized Crime has it from here. Want to go get lunch?"

"Uhh, yeah, sure."

The corporal nodded casually like the invite wasn't the

most shocking part of Green's day so far. "You know where Roman's Ramen is?"

He had only a vague idea. "Isn't that over in Claw sector?"

"Yep. It's fine, though. You're with me."

Don't blow this, Norman!

"Yeah, that sounds good."

"Cool, see you over there in fifteen, Rookie."

It wasn't until Green was already out of sector that he remembered an important tidbit about Roman's Ramen. Like most local businesses in Claw, it was werewolf owned and operated. But what was more, it was essentially patronized entirely by werewolves.

So, while it made sense as an establishment Bannockburn would enjoy, as a human, being surrounded on all sides by that particularly lethal type of creature was pants-dampening just to think about.

You're a cop, Norman! Act like it!

He supposed there wasn't likely to be anything of mention that arose from his creatural interloping when he was in uniform *and* accompanied by a werewolf in uniform.

Bannockburn was waiting in his car when Green pulled up next to him and parked, and the two casually walked up to the small restaurant nestled in a strip mall a few blocks off the highway. A neon sign glowed above the entry: a blue bowl with orange noodles heaped over the rim as alternating squiggles of steam flashing back and forth. It was like a beacon to hungry travelers who needed salt and carbs and protein—and quick.

It didn't surprise Green that this restaurant was open so late. With the bars open all night, Kilhaven's late-night cuisine options were many. But it did seem strange how full the place was for one a.m. on a weeknight.

As they approached the vacant hostess stand, a dark-skinned man peeked through the line window on the opposite wall and hollered to Bannockburn, who waved casually as he led Green over to an empty booth. The restaurant was dim, lit more like a bar than a restaurant, and immediately a beautiful young waitress approached and smiled. "Hey, Uncle Bruce."

Bannockburn grinned. "Oh, hey, Callie. Your parents let you work nights now?"

She shrugged. "Only when Haskel schedules me nights and no one will pick up my shift." She turned to Green. "Hi, can I get you something to drink?"

"Just water please," he said, grabbing a menu off the table and gluing his eyes to it. He couldn't shake the feeling that this one-on-one lunch date with the corporal was a test run of some sort, and he was determined not to blow it by accidentally checking out Bannockburn's underage niece.

"You like beef?" Bannockburn asked.

"Yep," replied Green.

The corporal turned to Callie. "Two of my usual, then."

Callie left, and Bannockburn reached across the table, lowering Green's menu. "I saved you the trouble. It's all basically the same thing, you know. Ramen. It's just noodles in broth with some meat and a bunch of shit you can't taste over the salt."

"Yeah, I know that," Green said, tucking the menu back behind the condiment caddy.

"All the same, I appreciate the effort you put into not ogling my niece."

"That wasn't why ..."

Bannockburn cut him off with a sharp clearing of his throat as he leaned back in the booth, throwing his arms up over the seat in a posture Green had become all too familiar with as the only way to relieve the constant pinching of the duty belt on one's intestines. He leaned back as well, though he clasped his hands on the table instead of making himself quite so at home in a werewolf establishment.

Bannockburn stared casually but unblinkingly at Green for a moment, then said, "They might end up calling the poncho thing the Green Protocol, you know."

"God, I hope not."

"I think we both know that the most important thing about the incidents, though, is purple, not Green."

Clenching his teeth together to wait patiently for Bannockburn to explain, Green's heart beat like a bass drum in his ears, drowning out the clamor of the crowded room around him.

"You've seen that purple before, Green, haven't you?" The corporal leaned forward then, setting his clasped hands on the table.

Green didn't move an inch. "Yes, sir."

Bannockburn shook his head minutely, softly shutting his eyes. "No, no, no. No calling me 'sir' right now, Green. Forget about us being cops. This is more important than that. Where have you seen that purple before?"

Was this a trap? Was Bannockburn doing this on behalf of Montoya? Maybe even on behalf of those above Montoya, the ones who made the call on firing Corporal Knox when she'd made that report of the vampire killing?

But then he remembered the look that passed between Valance and Bannockburn in show-up earlier that evening. It'd been unmistakably conspiratorial.

He mustered up the courage to answer his corporal honestly. "Saw it at Shady Grove the night before Knox was fired and you came on."

"And the circumstances?"

Did he say what he believed happened, or did he go for the answer he'd provided, with Valance's prompting, at his board review?

Think, Norman.

"Why did you bring me out of sector to a werewolf restaurant to ask me about this?"

A small smile crept onto Bannockburn's face. "You're not as stupid as Valance says."

"Thanks."

"You might benefit from catching up on a little local history, though." Bannockburn leaned back again. "Particularly the history of the Crown Tree neighborhood."

Green groaned. "I know a little *recent* history of it that's still working its way through the courts."

It took a moment, then Bannockburn's pinched brows relaxed. "Oh, you mean your shooting? Psh. Please. IA cleared you with a minor slap on the wrist. Grand jury packed with shifters is *not* going to side with an armed human. Not in Kilhaven. No, I mean more distant history. Particularly, the old families of Kilhaven. Like mine." He flashed a forced grin. "You much interested in politics, Green?"

"Not at all."

"Good for you. And I don't blame you, honestly. Not like a human could ever rise in the ranks. Shit is so corrupt, it's no wonder this country is going to hell in a handbasket. Goddamn vamps sit in their ivory towers making decisions for the masses they'd prefer to see annihilated. Think they're better than the rest of us."

And there it was. It made sense why they were at Roman's Ramen. Talk like that could get a person, especially a government employee, knee deep in shit if anyone mentioned it.

However, Green got the impression that this was a place where werewolf gossip was free to roam without fear of it leaving the building.

The corporal continued. "The Bannockburns were at the Battle of Everfield. Nearly decimated our line, but thankfully, we breed like were-rabbits and were able to carry on with the few survivors we had, mixing with families like the Kings and Valances and Silvertons."

"No offense, but why are you telling me this?"

Bannockburn leaned forward, his forearms flat on the tabletop. Flecks of gold and amber were visible in his brown irises at such proximity. "Because, Green—"

"Here you go." Callie set down two waters and two bowls of ramen. Hot broth sloshed over the edge of one, nearly splashing up into Bannockburn's face as he leaned so close to the tabletop. "Anything else I can get you?" she asked.

Now Green couldn't help but stare. Nothing like the bad timing of a teenage girl to ruin a moment. As a teenage boy, he'd experienced that plenty. Or maybe that'd been *him* ruining the moment. Yeah, probably that.

"We're good," Bannockburn said, smiling innocently at his niece before she hurried away.

The corporal grabbed his chopsticks and dug into his noodles immediately, pulling out a wad and blowing on it. "Damn, I love ramen."

But Green wasn't ready to dig in. "Uh, sir? You were saying something?"

Bannockburn shoveled the noodles into his mouth, biting off the hanging ends and sucking in air to cool the scalding food. He held up a finger and Green waited patiently.

When he was good and ready, Bannockburn wiped the droplets of broth from his face with his cloth napkin and resumed where he left off, much less intensely than before. "Right, right. As I was saying, my folks fought at all the big battles, and because of that, they got to be at the signing of the Treaty of Hornstooth. We go way back. Not just that couple hundred years, but even further. Back in the days when there *was* no civilized government, when wolves and vamps settled our differences with claw and talon, not parchment and ink. And even before that, when vamps hadn't yet washed up on our shores, rejects of their homelands, to become our problem.

"Those perverts have been around for a while, and they've caused trouble since the moment they got here. You think some dumb, outdated treaty is going to stop them from being the creeps that they are?"

Green stirred his soup listlessly with his chopsticks. "I guess not."

"Psh. Damn right." He shoved another steaming hunk into his mouth and added some of his ice water, swishing it around and then lumping the food into the side of his cheek. "More than doubtful. Anyone with half a brain knows it's just goddamn impossible. And anyone who's been raised with the stories of the depravities of those pedophile bloodsuckers knows it's worth doing whatever it takes to stop them."

He nodded at Green's bowl. "Eat your food."

Green did, shoving a bite into his mouth with minor difficulty—the Green family had stuck strictly to fork-and-steak-knife cuisine—then nodded and moaned as the flavor hit his brain.

Bannockburn jabbed his chopsticks at Green. "The point is that I know what I'm talking about, see? Best if you listen to me."

"Can I ask you something?"

"Just did."

"No, I mean, something else."

"Shoot, Rookie."

"Do you believe Corporal Knox's report from Shady Grove?"

Bannockburn sniffed curtly, his eyes falling to the condiment caddy as he paused. Then he met Green's eyes. "Better question: How far are you willing to go to do this job right?"

Trying to assess Bannockburn's meaning was tricky, but in the end, Green's gut told him that he was in trustworthy company. "What do you mean by right?"

The corporal's penetrating expression cracked, and he exhaled a single chuckle. "The kind of right that can get you fired and more."

Green wound a nest of noodles around his chopsticks then paused. "I think I answered that question up in Crown Tree. Answered it so clearly they gave me some time off." As he stuffed his mouth, burning his tongue and subsequently pretending he hadn't burned his tongue, Bannockburn erupted into laughter.

"Damn straight you did. Hopefully, we can go a little

longer than eight weeks with this thing before our heads are on the chopping block."

Green nodded, his eyes watering from the scalding, as the reality of what had just transpired in their conversation sank in.

Oh shit, did I just pick a side?

It sure as hell seemed that way, even though Bannockburn hadn't said as much.

Green finished chewing and blinked away a tear.

If he was going to take a side, though, the one with the terrifying power of Valance and Bannockburn was about as good a side as any.

CHAPTER SEVEN

Green's pager buzzed on his hip as he stood next to the ambulance where two frustrated paramedics treated a tight-lipped shifter stab victim who refused to provide even the most basic medical information. As Green pulled it off his belt to check, he noticed Brooks a few yards away, having just loaded the suspect into her vehicle, reaching for her belt, too. Must be a shift- or sector-wide page.

Green read off the short line of text. It indicated that he should check for a department email that contained an important message.

And, yet again, Green wondered why they even bothered with pagers.

He pulled out his phone from his back pocket and opened up his work email, waiting impatiently for the painfully slow 2G network to load his inbox.

He spotted it right away at the top of the heap of subject lines like, *Looking for a man who can show me* ... and *Your new favorite blade has arrived—but it will sell out soon!*

It was a message from Chief Spinner with the subject line of: *Regarding Recent Events.*

As he read through the information, he became more and more skeptical of what he was being told, regarding, specifically, the recent *explosion* events. It had been two long weeks after the Irishman popped in Green's lap like a purple slime balloon before the department addressed the issue publicly. Green assumed that meant leadership meetings had been a circus and no one had the slightest clue what to do moving forward. And once he read the email, his suspicions were all but confirmed. And not only that, it was obvious they still didn't have a clue how to address the situation.

The email contained a memo from Organized Crime, who stated that they suspected the cause of the explosions to be a drug manufactured and distributed by the cherubim. The chief then encouraged officers to keep an eye out for escalating tension between the cherubim and leprechauns.

It was the complete omission of vampires that left Green wondering if maybe Organized Crime wasn't giving the whole story.

Shit. Am I becoming paranoid?

Maybe vampires had nothing to do with it, but the purple connection was conspicuously overlooked time and again. Valance had even brought it up in that special way she had at shift meeting the night before, and Green had been somewhat surprised when it was Bannockburn who'd told her to give it a rest rather than Montoya. And he'd been downright shocked when Valance had actually listened.

Brooks strolled up, her phone in her hand, the screen still lit. "'Bout time we heard something from Organized Crime, right?"

Green kept his mouth shut but nodded agreeably.

"At least now you know it's not just you that makes things go splat." She giggled and then snorted at her own joke, and Green laughed along uncomfortably. "Anyway. These things heat up and then fall back into remission. The cherubim and leprechauns are at each other for now, but then it'll be the imps and pixies, and Demon sector will have to deal with that, or the harpies and necromancers over in Banshee, and we'll get a break for a little while."

Officer Tara Marrow walked over after wrapping up an interview with a witness. "You check this out yet?" She held up the pager.

Brooks caught her up to speed, then added, "Just telling the rookie how we'll get a break before long."

"You know what I could really use a break from," Marrow said, shaking her head exhaustedly, "is Valance and whatever conspiracy theory she's on about."

"Amen," said Brooks.

"Wait," Green said, "you both think she's crazy?"

Brooks cast him a pitying glance and placed a hand on his shoulder. "I know you two have a special relationship, but she has a tendency to go off the deep end every so often. You haven't been around long enough to see it yet, but it's about every year and a half she gets going on something—usually vamps—and just like with the gang wars, you gotta let it run itself out."

Marrow added, "And she's a few months overdue, actually."

Brooks let her hand drop from Green's shoulder. "Not everyone handled coming back from the war as gracefully as I have, Rookie. Nothing against the woman. But it is what it is."

"You don't believe any of it?" Green asked.

"Of course not," Marrow said. "But it is sort of nice that we have Bannockburn around this time to put her in her place."

Marrow and Brooks locked eyes and chuckled.

"What? What is it?" Green asked, trying to get a read on either of them. "What's so funny?"

Brooks arched a brow at him. "Green. Have you ever seen Valance let a man shout her down like that?"

"No, I guess not, but—"

"Why might she let a man do that, then?"

Obviously, he wasn't going to explain to these two that Valance and Bannockburn were onto something big, something dangerous, something that Green was suddenly knee-deep in himself. "Because they're cousins?"

For some reason, Officers Marrow and Brooks found that amusing. "*Distant* cousins," Brooks added.

Marrow clipped her pager back onto her duty belt. "Try not to be too jealous, Green."

"Huh? Jealous of what?"

Brooks nodded at Marrow, and the two of them turned and went back to their cars as Green hollered after them, "Jealous of what?" but got no answer back.

Instead, Brooks hollered over her shoulder. "Looks like it might rain. Better keep that poncho at the ready."

———

Hot droplets thumped the top of the cruiser like an angry mob punching its way in. The headlights of Green's vehicle cut through the rain as he pulled up to the address indicated on the HAM. He grabbed the bare minimum he needed, which wasn't much for a call like this, thankfully, and tried not to appear hurried as he hurried up to the stone archway on the doorstep of the Crown Tree home.

The father, Angelo Holloway, answered. He was black, not unlike Green's own father, which he acknowledged as a uniquely human observation. Mr. Holloway had been the one who called in the missing person, and it became clear why he, and not the mother, had done so as soon as Green made it into the large, nicely furnished living room. Or maybe people like this called it a parlor.

"Mrs. Holloway. I'm Officer Green with Kilhaven Police."

She was white, like his mother.

In his hometown of Bowers, this marriage might be something to talk about, but, thank Jesus or Dracula or whoever, he wasn't in Bowers anymore. Instead, he was in Kilhaven, where the bigger scandal was that Mr. Holloway was a werewolf, and Mrs. Holloway was fully human.

"Have a seat, officer," Angelo Holloway said, motioning toward a couch with a low, arched back and peach fleur-de-lis fabric.

He sat stiffly, adjusting his belt to keep it from rupturing his intestine, and Mrs. Holloway jumped up, proclaiming, "I'll make tea!" before scurrying off to the kitchen.

"You'll have to excuse her," Angelo said, "she was running late to pick up Caitlin from school, and she blames herself. But I'm sure you can help us, right?"

This was going to be one of *those* cases, wasn't it? Green had only had a couple so far in his career. They were the ones that haunted you at night, that created new, senseless, exposed triggers in your psyche, so you couldn't look at chocolate sprinkles without thinking of the maggots crawling on a teen mother's mangled and discarded corpse right off the highway.

Fuck, I need to stop thinking about that.

Green pulled out his notepad. "Can you tell me a little bit about your daughter, sir?"

"Caitlin," Angelo replied. "Caitlin Elizabeth Holloway. She's ten years old and— Well, here. Here's a picture of her." He reached forward and pulled from a stack on the coffee table, holding it out for Green, who took it and spun it around to get a good look.

He felt his heart jump in his chest. For a split second, he thought he was looking at a picture of his little sister, Kim. The similarities were startling, from the same slightly buck-toothed grin to the way they wore their hair.

Green nodded. "She's a beautiful girl, sir. I'll do everything I can to make sure she gets home safely."

Tears gathered in Angelo's eyes, but his face was stone except for a small muscle in his jaw that flexed and relaxed repeatedly.

"I'm going to ask you some questions. A few might upset you, but I have to ask them anyway if we want to get her home as quickly as possible."

"I understand. And it might be best if you jump straight to the difficult ones before my wife comes back in."

Green nodded and flipped to a fresh page in his notepad. "Has your daughter been in any trouble at school lately?"

"None I've heard of."

"Do you know if she has any friends who might get her into trouble?"

"She doesn't really have friends."

"Oh? Any particular reason you can think of?"

"Well, yes, actually." Mr. Holloway tilted his head toward Green. "You might be intimately familiar with it."

"People care about being mixed race here?" Green asked. Immediately the paranoia hit. Had everyone in KPD been talking about Green being biracial without him knowing it?

But Mr. Holloway shook his head adamantly, his brows low over his dark eyes. "Hell no. I just mean she's human. Almost every other kid at Prairie Peak elementary is timberwere or at least something besides human."

"What makes you say that with certainty, Mr. Holloway? She's only ten. There's always the chance that she could take after your side."

He shut that down with a wave of his hand. "She's not mine. She's Heather's first husband's. He was human. The odds of them producing anything else are so low it's not even worth considering."

"But it *does* happen," Green insisted. "So, is there any possibility that Caitlin experienced her first change and took off?"

Angelo seemed to consider it, but then cringed and shook his head. "No, she was always a little young for her age. I don't see her anywhere close to puberty."

"I understand."

This wasn't looking good. The sound of Heather Holloway moving around in the kitchen reminded him to get going with the tougher questions.

"Sir, is there anyone who you suspect might have taken your daughter, either believing she needed a ride or for nefarious purposes?"

"Oh sure," he said. "I'm running for city council, and a lot of people don't like that. Could have been one of them."

"What do you mean exactly? Why don't people like that?"

"Well, my mother was a Silverton. Not a name many people want in power."

That name rang a bell, but where had he heard it? He decided to play dumb, which was easy enough for him. Some would say he was an expert in it.

"Who wouldn't want you in power? Can you name names?"

Angelo suddenly jerked back a fraction of an inch, and Green could feel the man pulling away and shutting down. Flecks of amber shined in Mr. Holloway's eyes as he narrowed them at Green. "I don't have specific names. Just, you know, people in power who don't want to relinquish it to a werewolf." He watched Green closely as he spoke, then added, "Especially not a Silverton."

Green kept his composure which was, again, easy to do since he couldn't make much sense of the significance Mr. Holloway was attaching to this. He jotted down what he could, and as he was underlining *Silverton* and adding a note of *ask Valance*, Mrs. Holloway entered with the tea.

She set the tray down on the coffee table next to the pile of photos and then lowered herself onto a stiff chair next to her husband. "I realized halfway through making it that you might think I was up to something, what with you being a cop *and* a human *and* mixed race. It's quite impressive you've chosen this path despite how many people already hate you just for being alive."

Green blinked. "Thanks."

"I didn't pour the water. You can choose whatever cup you want so you don't think I've poisoned it, and I'll drink before you, and you can open the tea bag yourself."

Green forced a smile. Department policy discouraged accepting food or drinks, but after all the effort she went to, and because she was having such a rough day with her daughter missing, he figured the gesture of drinking the damn tea outweighed the risk of her having poisoned it. He reached forward and grabbed the cup farthest away from him on the tray. "That's very thoughtful. I'm not concerned about it," he lied.

Her eyes opened wide. "Oh, but you should be!"

"Should I?"

She nodded while Mr. Holloway cringed.

"Oh yes," she continued. "There are horrible people out there, Officer Green. You of all people ought to know, considering you're basically the bottom of the food chain in every community."

"I don't know about that."

"No, I get it," she said, holding a hand to her heart. "I'm a human, too. And I've lived the small human-town life *and* the city life. You strike me as someone who came from a small town."

He tried not to take offense and poured himself some tea as a distraction. "Yes, ma'am."

"Then you know how horrible people are. Human, shifter, werewolf, vampire—"

"Heather," Mr. Holloway interrupted.

She stared daggers at her husband. "What? I'm just saying, it's all alike. Everyone is horrible, and now our daughter is missing because of it."

Green set his tea on the green and blue mosaic side table to his left. "It sounds like you suspect someone took her, Mrs. Holloway. Is that what you suspect?"

Heather Holloway opened her mouth to reply, but Mr.

Holloway's firm hand on her knee tripped her up just long enough for him to jump in. "We don't know what happened to our daughter. And we don't care, as long as we get her home safe. She's only a child. She shouldn't be out there at two in the morning in the rain. She should be at home in bed."

Green nodded. It was true. And in the world of Should, it would be the reality. But over the past five months of police work, Green had boarded a ferry and was slowly setting sail away from the land of Should on a one-way journey to the twin islands of Is and Wish It Weren't. He hadn't quite lost sight of the shoreline of Should, but when a call like this came through, it was like a fog rolling in, temporarily obscuring any sign of the mainland.

And when he bid adieu to the Holloways, taking a couple photos of young Caitlin that would be projected onto every substation screen for show-up BOLOs over the coming days, he began to wonder if, when the fog thinned and the sun shone through, there would be any trace of a coastline left at all.

CHAPTER EIGHT_

While it was nice to be out of the rain for a few hours and enjoy a momentary distraction from the dread that Caitlin Holloway was already dead somewhere, Officer Green wished this buck-naked asshole would just stop running.

Or, at the very least, that the man would have picked a less creepy building to break into than Kilhaven First Draculan Church. The whole place felt like a macabre funeral home with the black walls, long hallways lit only by LED torches, and decorative coffins placed in each corner.

The suspect rounded one of said corners too quickly, sliding and clipping the edge of a coffin, which toppled over into Green's path. The lid slammed shut just before Green hurdled it.

"Police! Stop!" he called for the tenth time.

And it proved as effective as the previous nine times as the nude man kept on running, sock feet muffling his frantic footsteps on the crimson marble floors.

Green got eyes on the suspect again. "Hands where I can see them!" Immediately, he questioned the logic of his own words. What, did he think the man would draw a weapon on him? From where?

But it worked, and the suspect paused this time, turning to face the officer.

Only one hand was raised, though. The other reached behind and appeared again holding a wallet.

Dear God.

The wallet hit Green right in the chest, and in the time it took him to recoil and step away from the unsanitary object, the suspect was off again, taking a left where the hallway teed.

Green turned the corner just in time to see the door to the stairs slam shut.

"Shit." He grabbed his radio that was clipped to his shoulder. "Fang 9-07. He's heading up the stairs." Multiple officers from the Fang 900s had arrived on scene almost simultaneously, pulling into the empty parking lot with lights on. The call had started as a tripped alarm, but when a call came in from a neighbor that she'd just seen a large man enter the church in nothing but sock feet, two more units assigned to the call. Naked with sock feet was a clear indicator of a bad drug reaction, and that often took a team effort to handle.

But the church was huge, so the obvious approach was to fan out. Green had been doubled up with Lawrence until they hit a fork and decided to split. By now, Green's backup could be anywhere in the gigantic building that seemed constructed as a maze for rats.

Green charged forward to the stairs, gun aimed out at the floor ahead. Thanks to his subpar sense of smell, Green hadn't yet gotten close enough to the suspect to tell what creature he was dealing with, except he suspected that if the man were a shifter or a werewolf, he would have changed already. And he was too tall to be a leprechaun or cherub, thankfully. But that still left quite a few options. He could be a human, a telepath, a telekinetic (although, if the latter were the case, Green might already be dead), a warlock, or any other number of strange things Green had yet to encounter but had learned about through a single projected slide in the academy.

Regardless of what the man was, he was definitely skilled at evading arrest.

"Fang 9-13," Lawrence called back, "I'm on the third floor. 9-01, what's your location?"

"Waiting on the fourth floor," Valance replied. "Eyes on the stairwell."

Green pursued up the stairs. At least he knew the subject wasn't armed. Sure, the wallet stunt had shaken this belief somewhat, but a flat wallet and a knife or gun were entirely different when it came to cramming them up your ass. So, yes, it was possible the man had stashed his wallet *and* a small pistol in his bum, but a pistol, at least, would take a good bit of finagling to dislodge, and Green would be ready for it.

He heard a door slam not far above him. "Suspect left the stairwell."

"Clear on three."

"Clear on four."

Shit. "Must be on two," Green replied, sprinting up the flight and pausing before the door to get his head on straight in case of an ambush. He really hoped he didn't have to shoot this guy. Two shootings in less than a year, regardless of how justified, would for sure lose him his job. Against his better judgment, he holstered his firearm and drew his Taser before creeping out of the stairwell, looking both ways down the long, dark hall.

He caught the faintest glimpse of a shadow at the far end. "He's on two," he radioed before taking off at a sprint.

The question wasn't so much whether the man was on drugs as it was *what drugs is this lunatic on?* It was rarely just one with calls like this. Regardless, so long as he didn't shift to something with a thick skin, the Taser would do the trick until Green could slap on cuffs and this exhausting pursuit could come to an end.

A heavy door slammed somewhere beyond Green's line of sight, and he cursed and paused. A moment later, Lawrence and Valance crept out of the stairs behind him. He turned to them. "He must have gone into one of the rooms. Either of you get a read on him?"

Valance nodded. "More like he got a read on us. Telepath. I could feel his wired brain reaching. He'll manage to keep the drop on us all night, so long as he can read where we are."

She and Lawrence exchanged a look, and Lawrence nodded. "Flush him out?" he said.

"Yep." She turned to Green. "Guess you're not dead weight after all, Rookie. Head downstairs and wait by the elevator. We'll send you a little gift."

"Sealed with a fucking kiss," Lawrence added, then he crept forward, Valance by his side, and Green did as he was told, going back down to the first floor to wait by the elevator.

Waiting in a place like this was inarguably worse than sprinting through it. It was dead silent. Unlike the higher levels of this building, the first floor was covered with short, bristly crimson carpet rather than marble, further dampening any noise. If it were still raining outside, he couldn't hear it. But the worst part of the silence was when it was broken by a creak or an unexplained pop, originating somewhere down the tomb-like hallways. He squinted into the darkness, struggling to remain calm. How did Officer Harmon stand worshipping in a place like this? How did anyone? Well, vampires he could understand. They loved this creepy shit.

The grind of gears and creak of cables caused Green to whirl toward the elevator, putting his back to the dark, empty hallway. The light-up sign to the top left of the door indicated that it had stopped on the second floor. After a heavy silence the noise kicked up again, and a down arrow indicated the elevator was heading Green's way.

He sidestepped, making sure he wasn't immediately visible when the doors first parted, before he could put eyes on the suspect. If the man felt pinned, which he was about to be, there was no telling what he might try. Green's best chance was to catch the suspect by surprise the moment he set foot in the hallway.

Not two steps clear of the sliding door, and Green brought the man to the ground as swiftly as possible, which wasn't all that swift and included a few failed attempts to swipe the legs that meant Green was simply kicking the man in the shins. But the result was the same, and the pain of a boot or three to the fibula was enough to crumple the telepath, despite whatever concoction of drugs he was on.

Green snapped on the cuffs and, once he had the suspect pinned firmly underneath his knee—thankfully, facedown with his loose junk squished against the carpet—he radioed for the others to join him.

"What'd I do?" the suspect demanded. "I didn't do nothing!"

"Sir, you broke into a church in the middle of the night wearing nothing but socks. I should be asking *you* what you did."

"Nothing!" the man protested. "I ain't done nothing!"

"Except cocaine? Feed? What are you on?"

The suspect wiggled and twitched underneath Green's knee. "I don't do drugs!"

"That makes your behavior even weirder, sir. Man to man, I suggest you blame it on the drugs."

Lawrence and Valance ran up the hallway away leading from the stairwell and helped Green pull the suspect to standing.

He glared at Valance. "So *you're* the angry fucker I was reading." He grinned, his lips curling to reveal a mostly toothless sliver of a grin.

"I'm not angry," Valance said, reaching into a pocket on the back of her belt and pulling out a folded-up iron-threaded cap.

"You are when you fuck," said the suspect. "I saw that plain enough."

She shoved the heavy fabric over his head. "You should know that reading the thoughts of a law enforcement officer with the intent to exploit, bait, or evade arrest is a state jail felony."

His mouth fell open, and when he tried to shake off the cap that impeded his telepathy, Valance leaned forward, grabbed the two strings hanging loosely on either side of his chin, and tied them together in a square knot beneath his jaw

As the rush subsided, a sharp pain in Green's throat

when he tried to swallow triggered a very recent memory of the suspect elbowing him in the neck. His pulse pounding through his jugular renewed the pain in small but persistent jolts.

Valance kept her composure in every visible way except the one she couldn't control: her eyes. They were glowing amber, which Green took as an indication that she was on the edge of beating the ever-living crap out of the suspect. That meant it was best if he handed off the suspect to Lawrence, who accepted him into his custody without question, leading the naked man out through the front doors of the church.

A fourth car had arrived sometime between when they'd entered the church and when they emerged again, and it wasn't until the door opened and the occupant stepped out that Green could see who it was.

"What the hell's he doing here?" Green whispered to Valance.

She didn't seem at all surprised or interested, though, in the appearance of Sergeant Montoya on scene. "He probably got tired of sitting on his ass all day and wanted to come see the show." She glanced at Green, who was absentmindedly rubbing his throat. "You gonna make it?"

"Huh? Oh, yeah. Just got an elbow to the neck back in there."

"Fondling your exposed throat like that in a vampire church parking lot is just asking for it, you know."

Green didn't agree with the sentiment but decided not to press that specific point. "It doesn't seem weird to you that Sarge showed up? It's a Friday night. The rain is probably the only thing keeping this city from burning itself to the ground. An armed robbery call came through right as I pulled up here."

She elbowed him in the chest. "You're overthinking it, Rookie."

Sergeant Montoya met the three officers and the suspect under the awning. "Everything good?"

"Besides this man's rug-burned dong," Lawrence replied, "yeah, it's all good."

The sergeant looked the suspect in the eyes. "What's your name?"

"George."

"What were you doing in there, George?"

"Just getting out of the rain, sir."

"And why are you naked?"

"My clothes were soaked. I just wanted to dry off for a little while. I don't got no home."

Valance groaned. "I eagerly await the made-for-TV film based on your tragic life." She glanced at Montoya. "Can I get out of here? It's a strain on my virginity to be around such an impressively chaffed and flaccid cock."

Montoya grimaced. "For the love of ... Yes, just go." He turned to Green. "You can head out, too. I'll catch up with Lawrence and take this man down to jail myself."

Lawrence appeared as confused as Green, but Valance acted as though she couldn't care less and walked back to her car without another word. Unsure of what else there was to say, and not wanting to risk saying anything that accidentally got him stuck with the report and a late-shift trip down to jail, Green kept his mouth shut and jogged through the rain back to his car asap.

Once he was inside and glimpsed the time, he realized it

was only twenty minutes until he could head back to the substation. Too much time to do nothing, and not enough time to handle any single call without ending up pulling overtime.

Most nights ended with overtime for him since he was the only rookie on the shift and was therefore left with all the last-minute bullshit calls. He didn't mind it on the whole; at the rates they paid first-year officers, the extra cash provided a nice financial cushion. But on a night like tonight, when the rain was relentless and his mind was swimming with anxieties and unknowns, spending sunrise asleep in his bed rather than typing up reports was much more desirable.

He cut across the parking lot, idly browsing the calls on the HAM, hoping none couldn't wait another half hour until day shift was ready to handle them when a message came through from the car behind him: *Your trunk is open, Rookie.*

It was from Valance.

Dammit.

He pulled off into an auto parts parking lot on the other side of the road, preparing to sprint around in the rain, hope nothing was ruined from the water, and then run back around.

But before he could make a break for it, a hard rap on the passenger's side window drew his attention, and Valance's face stared back at him. He hurriedly unlocked the door, and she jumped in, slamming it shut behind her.

"What are you—"

She slapped a hand over his mouth and began disabling his equipment, starting with the dash cam, and ending with his body mic.

"Radio that you're having technical difficulties."

"Huh?"

"Your equipment is malfunctioning. You're going to see if you can fix it, but you're unable to take another call before you head in."

"Wait, what?"

"Don't be a dense twat. Just fucking do it."

Green nodded slowly and radioed. "Fang 9-07. My recording equipment and HAM just lost power. Gonna see if I can't fix the issue, but I might have to bring it back into the substation."

Corporal Bannockburn's voice was the first to come through. "Fang 9-80 to 9-07. I had that happen just the other day. Try shutting off the car for a bit and then starting it again. Sometimes that resets the equipment."

Green turned to Valance. "That works?"

She wiped a tired hand over her face. "No, of course not. Bannockburn is covering, you idiot."

"Oh. Covering for what?"

She placed a hand on the door handle, her body language telling him she was halfway out of the car already, and she paused. "You know, I'm rethinking getting you on our side. If you want to hop on the vampires-are-awesome-and-harmless bandwagon, I wouldn't be heartbroken."

Oh. That's what this was about. Maybe he would have caught on sooner if his night hadn't left him so preoccupied. Maybe not. "No, no. I'm with you. Why are you in my car?"

She let go of the handle slowly, narrowing her eyes at him. "Yeah, I guess we need everyone we can get. Besides, you know too much already." She sucked a chestful of air in through her nose and turned to face him directly. "That missing persons call you went to earlier. Anything?"

Green reached in the center console and pulled out the

photos, handing them to Valance. "Caitlin Holloway. Father Angelo Holloway is running for—"

"City council." Valance flipped quickly through the three photos the Holloways had sent along. "Idiot. What'd he think would happen if he stuck his neck out around vampires?" She tossed the photos into Green's lap.

"Does the name Silverton mean anything to you?"

Not surprisingly, Valance frowned, cocked her head to the side and looked at him like he was stupid. "Of course it does. One of the original timberwere families. Fought at Everfield. Mostly died at Everfield. Why?"

"Holloway says his mother was a Silverton."

Valance gasped then gagged on her own spit, coughing until she regained the ability to breathe. "No shit? How is the news not all over that?" She cracked her knuckles and chewed on her lip. "This is gonna get uglier than I thought."

"Valance. What the hell is going on?"

"Those girls are never coming back, Green."

A stabbing pain in his chest told him that she was right. He stared down at the photo of Caitlin on a swing, laughing, happy. He thought of his sister, Kim.

"I don't know the specifics," Valance continued, "but I do know the vamps have them. And *if* we ever see those poor little girls again, they're not going to be the girls their parents loved. They'll be something much, much worse and bloodthirsty."

Whether because the thought of vampires stealing and murdering—or worse, *turning*—little girls was too much for him to bear or because Valance was acting overly jumpy and paranoid, Green wasn't yet convinced of the conspiracy she was hinting at. "Both girls were taken during the day. Even I know vampires don't fuck around in the daylight."

"That's why I said I don't know the specifics yet."

"Some people might instead argue it's why vampires *didn't* do it."

Valance set a warm hand on his thigh, and he tried not to flinch. "Listen, I know you don't want to believe this. I don't want to believe it either. But I do believe it. I believe it despite how much I don't want to believe it, and that should mean something. Do you trust me?"

He guessed "that depends" wasn't the right answer, so, for the sake of his own safety when Valance's hand was so near his tender bits, he said, "Of course."

"Bannockburn says he took you to lunch the other day and tried to make it clear to you what was going on but that you were remarkably dense. I told him that's pretty much par for the course. But since we need Bruce to keep rising in the ranks, we can't afford to risk his career just to be as obvious as you need us to be. So, here it is, all spelled out.

"Hornstooth isn't worth shit anymore. The only people who believe that treaty still exists are the ones who choose denial over reality. And the reality is that vampires can't control their own, and this whole town has been silently victimized because of it. It goes in waves. Two years ago, we had another rash of disappearing children, and only two were ever found. One was by me, the other by Bannockburn over in Ecto where he used to patrol. But as far as the *department* knows, none were ever found. You comprehend what I'm saying here?"

Green swallowed and nodded.

"A baby vamp is like a baby copperhead," Valance continued. "Bites whatever it can get its mouth on and goes overboard. If the truth trickled out that those missing timberwolf children had been turned by vamps, well, you can kiss what thin threads of law and order remain in this town goodbye. Kilhaven has been looking for an excuse to self-destruct for decades. As entertaining as that shitshow may be, you and I both know we can't let it happen, Green.

"So, for now, we say nothing. You understand? Nothing. Zero. Until I tell you otherwise, 'vampire' isn't even in your vocabulary and you fell asleep in class the day they taught about the Treaty of Hornstooth."

"What can we do, though? You just said if Kilhaven finds out, it'll self-destruct."

"It's complicated. Two years ago, we weren't expecting it. Bannockburn and I didn't have a clue, and we didn't have a single connection in leadership. He wasn't a corporal yet. But as we started to put together the pattern, we knew it'd come back, and now we're ready. If this is going to come to light, we have to be smart about it, figure out who we can trust, and come up with a strategy for notifying the public that the problem is handled at the same time we let them know it existed in the first place. And that's not easy. There are a lot of people in the department with ties to the elves who would leak the lead before we had it fixed. The plan is to get everything lined up before we bust this open, or else it'll just turn into another cover-up, or worse, it'll turn to riots. As big a heap of steaming excrement as the Treaty of Hornstooth was and still is, the war wasn't any prettier, and the last thing we need is weres and vamps going at it openly again. Nobody won that war the two hundred years ago, and nobody will win it now. Especially not with the weapons we have."

Green's heart raced as the rain continued to pound on the metal roof. "Okay. What's our move?"

Valance gripped his leg tighter and leaned forward. His

eyes felt like they were chained to hers. "Nothing right now. But when the time comes, I'll need you and whoever else I can recruit by my side."

"How will I know when that is?"

"I'll let you know. Until then, you say nothing to anyone, okay? Not even Bannockburn. You're not exactly subtle, and your stupidity could ruin everything, so I'm your only contact from here on out, understand?"

"Yes. But also, fuck you."

Her hand loosened its firm grasp but slid slightly higher up his thigh. "Don't you talk dirty to me, Rookie. If we play that game, I'll ruin you." She let go and leaned back in her seat. "The code word is 'sucker.' You hear me say that to you over the radio, you haul your ass to wherever I am. Understand?"

"Uh, sure."

Valance groaned and rolled her eyes. "I guess minimal verbal confirmation will have to do." She opened the door and paused. "Now plug in all your shit and head to the substation. If anyone asks, Bannockburn's suggestion worked."

She slammed the door shut behind her and Green was left alone.

Just as he was about to start the car again, a question niggled at him: was his trunk really open? His rearview mirror wasn't much help through the torrential rain, and while it looked like it was shut, he couldn't be certain.

So, he waited until Valance had pulled away then sprinted around to the back to check.

It was shut.

CHAPTER NINE_

"She's got a gun," Brooks whispered from beside the window of the decrepit doublewide.

"*She's* got a gun?" Green repeated back incredulously. "But I thought she was pregnant."

Brooks shot him a scornful look. "You haven't met a lot of pregnant women, have you?"

Beside Green, Officer Lawrence shifted anxiously on his heels. "I'm gonna go around to the back," he said.

Green and Brooks nodded, but before Lawrence took off, he paused, winced, and said, "Let's not the three of us shoot a pregnant shifter, okay?"

"Good idea," Brooks whispered back.

Green also thought it was a good idea.

The shouting amplified and Green nodded to Brooks before they darted the short distance to the front door. Brooks knocked and announced their presence.

From behind the thin door, clear as day, the woman's voice rang out. "You're gonna have to shoot me!"

"Oh, for fuck's sake," Brooks grumbled. "Ma'am," she shouted, "we don't want to hurt you. But we're coming in!"

She drew her weapon, and so did Green, then she nodded, and he set his feet, readying himself to kick down the door.

"No," she hissed, pushing him back a step. She grabbed the knob and it turned just fine.

Before they entered, Brooks radioed, "Fang 9-13 to 9-07. Come around the front."

A child had called in the disturbance, which meant, of course, that there was at least one child somewhere in the home. The immediate danger, though, was the incredibly pregnant woman holding the sawed-off shotgun at her boyfriend's chest between facing rows of fiberboard kitchen cabinets. The barrel was aimed away from the rest of the house toward an outside wall, so that, at least, was lucky when it came to child safety, though, obviously, the safest thing for children would be to not live around two adult psychos. But things being what they were, the coastline of Should had been left far behind.

"Ma'am, drop the gun," Brooks said in her sweet Southern drawl as she and Green moved to block the entrance to the kitchen. It wasn't ideal to corner the suspect —that was known to lead to more irrational behavior in distressed subjects—but there was no other choice in the cramped trailer.

"I already told you! You're gonna have to shoot me!"

While Brooks engaged the suspect, Green did a quick scan of the surroundings. Empty beer bottles and other unidentifiable detritus blanketed the countertops, and blackened pans balanced precariously in the sink. However this scene played out, Green couldn't help but feel that the baby on the way was doomed.

"The only reason we would have to shoot you," Brooks responded, "is if you turn the gun on us or pull that trigger on him. You can point the gun at him all day long, as far as I'm concerned, so long as you don't shoot."

The woman's nostrils flared slightly, and her lips tightened.

"Ma'am, this is Norman, and I'm Aliyah. We're just here to help you. I know you got your reasons to be pointing a gun at him, but we can talk about it. What's your name?"

Lawrence's boots announced his arrival behind Green, who took his eyes off the scene just long enough to mouth "children" and point down the hallway. Lawrence nodded and went to find however many might be hiding.

"Sophia."

Green remained at the ready, but his eyes flickered over to Brooks. God, he hoped she could make a miracle happen.

Slowly so as not to spook the woman, Green switched out his gun for his Taser.

Brooks's aim was that of someone who'd cut a sweet deal with the devil, and as warm and congenial as her presence seemed on first blush, he knew better by now. She wouldn't hesitate to fill a pregnant woman with lead if it came to that, which, from the perspective of a fellow officer was comforting to know whenever she arrived as his backup. But from the perspective of a fellow living being, the knowledge was more disturbing than he had the brain capacity to process at the moment.

If he had an opportunity to tackle her where she wouldn't get off a shot, Green would have to take it. Roughing up a pregnant woman in a room this cramped and cluttered could go poorly in a thousand unique ways, but at least Sophia stood a chance then. And so did her unborn baby.

Brooks nodded at the man who'd remained awfully quiet in his fitted jeans, pearl-snap shirt, and alligator boots. "What'd you do?" she asked.

"Huh?" his face filled with horror, and Green wondered if the man were reassessing any feminist statements he'd ever supported.

Brooks turned back to Sophia. "That your boyfriend?"

"He *was.*"

"Why don't you lower the gun and tell me what happened?"

"Why don't I keep it here and tell you what happened?"

Brooks remained calm, or as calm as someone could be while pointing a gun at someone else. "That's fine. Just please don't pull the trigger before we can get this sorted out. If not for your sake, for your baby's sake."

"It's his baby too. Maybe I don't care if she dies." But even as Sophia said it, her voice cracked, tears welled in her eyes, her shoulders slump an inch.

Brooks turned back to the man. "What's your name?"

"Donovan."

"Okay, Donovan. You love this woman?"

Donovan nodded adamantly.

Well, he's not a complete idiot.

"More than anything in this world?" Green prompted hastily, hoping Donovan would keep up the good work.

"More than anything in this world!"

Sophia's hands were shaking, which Green suspected was a good sign. Or, it could mean she was at the end of her rope.

Brooks was right; he did not understand pregnant women. His instructors hadn't included a slide on *that* in the academy, but they should have. He'd try to remember to recommend it to someone in charge later on.

"What'd you do, Donovan?" Brooks asked again.

"Nothing! I ain't done nothing!"

"Dude!" said Green quickly. "Come on here."

"Be honest," Brooks jumped in. "You did *something*. She's not overreacting. I can tell she's not like that. You have to have done something."

Donovan, with arms still raised, looked back and forth between the officers as if they were old friends hanging him up to dry. Then his eyes widened as his gaze fell to waist height between Green and Brooks.

Green hadn't even noticed the footsteps approaching. "Mama, please don't shoot Donovan," the child's thin voice begged. "I know he's bad, but please don't shoot him."

Sophia's hands shook in earnest, but she kept the barrel of the shotgun aimed at her boyfriend, only it'd started to sag in her hands and was leveled at his groin rather than his chest.

Green glared at Lawrence, wondering what the hell he was thinking, letting the three young boys anywhere near this familial clusterfuck. If shit went south, not only would IA have their asses, but victim services would also throw a fit, and for good reason.

Lawrence feigned an attempt at herding the boys out the door without accomplishing anything of note.

Brooks stepped into the kitchen. "Sophia, not in front of the children," she whispered. "You'll go to jail, and it'll be the last memory they have of you." Brooks holstered her weapon.

Sophia's body shook as the first sob issued from her. The barrel of the shotgun had hardly lowered two inches before Brooks was on her, snatching the gun from her hands and shoving it at Green in a smooth motion that caught him off guard and almost caused him to drop it as he fumbled to holster his Taser. Brooks had Sophia pressed against a countertop, wrists behind her and the silvers clicked on before there was any chance of resistance. But the woman was lost in tears, her whole body heaving with each sob. Only when she turned to look at her children did Green spot the deep purple and blue of a fresh black eye.

As Lawrence whisked all three boys away and to safety outside, Green set down the shotgun behind him and pointed his Taser at Donovan. "Hands up. Don't even think about shifting," Green said.

Judging by the shock on Donovan's face, he'd been only seconds away from doing that exact thing. Part of Green wished the dickhead would try it, so he had an excuse to tase him mid-shift. There were stories of that causing permanent damage to shifters, making them partially shifted for life. Though the department adamantly rejected those stories as urban legends, an officer could hope.

"I didn't do nothing!" Donovan protested as Green rushed him.

"We both know that's bullshit," Green hissed in his ear as he spun him around against the countertop and clicked on the silvers.

"I'm the victim here!" Donovan continued.

I could probably dry-fire the Taser into his back and claim it was a mistake. One, maybe two days suspension tops.

No, not worth it. Almost worth it. Pretty fucking close to worth it. But Valance would have his ass if he fucked up in such a dumb way when they were neck deep in something much more important.

Donovan moaned at the burn of the handcuffs against his skin. But Green had no sympathy to spare. Because, as usual, the woman with the gun turned out to be the victim. She'd simply gotten the upper hand in the end. And really, good for her.

Unfortunately, that didn't mean she wasn't in for a long night. There'd be the required hospital visit, speaking with a Family Violence detective, and social workers galore. Green suspected the law would overlook the fact that she'd almost killed a man, but you never really knew, did you?

While Sophia would likely get off scot-free, Donovan was going straight to jail then on to prison if Green had any say in the matter. It was never fun to arrest a parent in front of his or her children, but after months of it becoming a weekly occurrence, Green learned to cope. After all, he wasn't the one who decided to do drugs or beat people up or steal strangers' prosthetic limbs in front of children. The parents had made all those decisions, but, in the end, when the children decided it was too painful to believe their parents were the scumbags, Green would become the scapegoat.

Once Brooks had the full story from Sophia about the night's events leading up to the shotgun snafu (including a few too many beers and a few too many punches and accusations) and Green had scraped together a modest confession from Donovan, which differed wildly from his baby mama's story, the officers allowed themselves a moment to relax and breathe. Grandma was on her way for the children, and both Sophia and Donovan could use a little time in their respective backseats to think about the major life decisions that led them to this point.

"For future reference," Brooks said, standing next to Lawrence and across from Green, her hands clasped just above her duty belt, "most women just want to be listened to."

Green was at a loss. "Are we talking about what just happened, or …?"

Brooks shrugged. "In general. We basically spend our whole lives being told our emotions make us crazy. Then men go around fucking with our emotions non-stop because they know we feel guilty having them. Sometimes that results in us pointing a gun at a motherfucker. But usually, it results in us pointing a gun at ourselves."

Lawrence rolled his eyes. "Please, everyone knows the preferred method of suicide for women is poison or slitting wrists, not guns."

Brooks shoved him. "For fuck's sake. It's a metaphor."

"It didn't start out as a metaphor," Lawrence insisted. "It started out literal."

"Also," Green added, "you kept saying 'us' like you have emotions."

"Eh," Brooks conceded with a slight nod, "good point. Maybe I don't know what I'm talking about. Working special forces in the Amazon pretty much wrings the emotion out of you."

Lawrence said, "Take Valance, for example. She was special forces, right?"

Brooks grimaced and scrunched her nose. "I don't actually know. I think she was, like, extra special forces or something. Deep ops. I don't know if the government would even admit she worked for them. That kind of thing."

"Ah, yeah," Lawrence said. "That theory supports the paranoia, alright."

Green knew that he shouldn't, but he did anyway. "I don't know that she's necessarily paranoid."

The other two officers turned to face him directly, planting their boots in the gravel driveway, and he had a flash of sympathy for any suspect who ended up with Brooks and Lawrence interviewing them post-crime.

"You believe her," Brooks said, slightly amused. "Well, I guess it makes sense."

"What?" Green asked.

"That you believe her. She trained you, didn't she? A little brainwashing goes a long way. It happens."

Green decided the stupid card was the one to play. Apparently, most people thought he had a deck full of nothing else. Might as well exploit that. "I don't know what you're talking about. Believe her about what?"

But Brooks wasn't falling for it, and Lawrence's slightly cocked but no less perfectly sculpted eyebrow indicated he wasn't either.

"Starts with a V ends with you being fired," Brooks said sternly. Then she crinkled up her nose and turned to Lawrence. "That sounds like I mean vagina, doesn't it?"

He nodded.

"Well, I don't," she said to Green. "I mean that other thing. The dangerous one no one wants to talk about but basically runs everything."

"That could still be a vagina," Lawrence said.

Brooks grunted and leaned closer to Green, whispering, "Vamps."

"I take it you don't believe her?" Green said, not wanting

to incriminate himself. But while he expected a flat-out denial, that wasn't what he got.

Instead, Brooks hedged for a moment, shifting her feet. "I'm not saying I completely don't believe her. But what the hell's she gonna do about it? The most likely outcome is that crazy bitch gets herself fired, and that's the end of that."

"Do you believe her?" he asked Lawrence, who leaned and peered past the hood of his car to check on the children where they sat in the muddy front yard.

"Huh? Oh, you mean about the … *not* vaginas? Psh. Oh yeah. I totally believe Valance on that. Like, one hundred percent. It's totally obvious."

Green narrowed his eyes. "I can't tell if you're being sarcastic."

Lawrence folded his arms high across his chest. "Oh, no. I'm totally serious about this. I've seen it happening for years now. You'd kind of have to be blind or unbelievably stupid not to pick up on it, especially in a craphole of a sector like Fang where people get sloppy about their murders."

Green took a quick step back, holding up his hands defensively to slow the flow of information. "Wait, so you *agree* with Valance?"

Lawrence looked him straight in the eyes, and sure enough, there was no disingenuousness to his expression. "Totally." He looked back at the kids. "I just don't agree with her crusade to do something about it."

"Why not?"

Lawrence let his arms fall to his sides. "Because that's not our job. That's the job of the people above us. Our job is to run around being undertrained counselors and overqualified janitors. Valance just can't let her extra-special-ops days go. Is there a conspiracy at work here? Probably. Likely more than one. But I'm not going to be the one to put the pieces together and fix this mess, so, in the meantime, I'm gonna get paid."

"Damn." Something about Lawrence's sentiment struck a chord with Green but also repulsed him slightly. He nodded at Brooks. "And you feel the same?"

She didn't respond immediately as she stared distantly at the three kids sitting on the front lawn. "I guess I don't know how I feel." She snapped out of her trance and addressed Green directly. "Like I said, the war pretty much wrung out all my feelings." She flashed an empty smile. "I'm gonna escort this pregnant lady to the hospital to get checked out. Y'all try not to let those kids run in the street until Grandma gets here. Then you let them run in the street all you want."

Green's week since the stand-off in the kitchen had been a series of false alarms and civil disputes that in no way, shape, or form necessitated police involvement. It was maddening to both wish something interesting would happen but also know that "interesting" went hand-in-hand with "a danger to your continued existence."

Presently, Green sat in his cruiser in the Quick Z gas station parking lot, chipping away at the stolen vehicle report. Despite how basic the average person might assume a stolen vehicle call would be, as Green had learned, they were usually some of the biggest clusterfucks one could find.

They weren't dangerous so much as a web of lies upon lies. If the claim was, "a masked stranger ran up, broke the front window, and hot-wired the thing," the reality usually fell somewhere between "I crashed it into a pole drinking and driving last night and ditched it by the side of the road" and "my ex borrowed it to see his other lady who I told him I was cool with but am not cool with, and I'm looking to get him caught up in a felony traffic stop where he either wets himself or decides he has too many warrants and opens fire on the cops."

In the report Green was slogging through, the owner of the vehicle had allowed his drug dealer to hold his truck as collateral until the owner could sell off a large baggie of cocaine, earn the money back, pay the dealer, and have his vehicle returned.

Unfortunately, the owner of the vehicle had decided to do all the coke himself over a three-day binge.

It was a tedious report to type up, so when Valance's call sign came over the radio, Green listened up for an excuse to roll out.

He didn't have to wait long. "Fang 9-01. Just arrived on scene where the caller claims her husband has returned home. Should be noted he died about three weeks ago. No sign of the husband at the moment. May call for backup if he shows again."

Now, *there* was a call. Almost on a nightly basis, Green's natural instinct to assume that just because he'd seen a lot on this job meant he'd seen everything bit him in the ass. Was this a zombie call? He'd begun to assume the instructors at the academy had only told zombie stories to scare the cadets. But maybe there was some truth to them after all.

He returned to the HAM, typing furiously to finish his report in case Valance called for backup. He wanted to see a goddamn zombie.

Just as his eyes began to cross and his fingers typed the last few words that may or may not have been gibberish, more chatter came over the radio.

"Fang 9-01. I think I might have eyes on this sucker. Requesting backup."

"Fang 9-80. On my way," came Bannockburn's voice.

Well, shit, Green wasn't going to miss a zombie. The law allowed for shooting a zombie in the head without any legal repercussions. He wanted in on that.

"Fang 9-07. Same traffic."

He ran lights but no sirens until he reached the neighborhood, then he went all lights out the rest of the way until he pulled up to the address. No point hauling ass over if he'd just scare away the zombie before he could get a glimpse of it.

Corporal Bannockburn pulled up behind him and jogged up to approach with Green. "Worried you might miss the signal," Bannockburn said.

"The signal?"

"Oh, for cryin' out loud. You didn't even realize, did you?"

"Realize what?"

"Suckers?"

"What about— Oh. Right. I mean, yeah. I knew."

"No, you didn't. You thought this would be a zombie." He held out a hand to stop Green from entering through the open front door. "If she called us here, it isn't a zombie. Now I'll keep from mentioning this to her if you get your damn head on straight. We might have something serious."

Green nodded, and Bannockburn growled but dropped his arm and led the way into the rundown one-story home.

When they entered, they found Valance standing stiffly, hands clasped at her waist, on the far side of the living room. The female caller sat on a dingy couch with her back to the front door, and as they came around, Green noticed the dishrag she wrung in her clenched hands.

"This is Officer Green and Corporal Bannockburn," Valance said. "They're here to catch your husband."

The woman twisted on the couch cushion and her eyes followed Bannockburn as he walked around toward Valance. "You think he's a zombie, too?" the woman asked. "I swear, Stan down the street is a hardcore necromancer. I've known it all along."

Bannockburn crouched on the floor in front of her, bracing himself for balance on a metal side table and staring up into her eyes. "Ma'am, we don't know what is going on yet, but we'll handle it, don't worry. What I need you to do is stay calm. And show me a picture of your husband."

She pointed toward the wall where a cluster of picture frames hung off kilter. With a small grunt, Bannockburn raised himself to stand, hooked his thumbs into his belt, and crossed the tiny space, leaning close to inspect the photographs. "Ma'am, would you mind staying here for just a moment while I speak privately with these two officers?"

She sniffled. "Of course not."

The corporal tossed a look Valance's way, and she nodded, following him and Green to the doorstep and closing the door gently behind her. Bannockburn pointed at Green's chest, which meant nothing discernible to Green. But then both Bannockburn and Valance reached down and unclipped the tiny mics on the hems of their uniforms between the top two buttons, gently unplugging each. Green caught on and did the same, flinching when he jerked the cord out maybe a little too hard for it to go back in. Whatever, he'd deal with that later.

"You sure about this, Heather?"

Valance nodded. "Ran the name of this neighbor she claims is a necromancer. He's just your run-of-the-mill meth-head shifter. I can see why she might confuse the two, with both active all night long, but I don't buy it."

"That's all you got?"

Valance froze, her nostrils flickering wider for a fraction of a second. "No, that's not *all*. The wife says he worked at Decatur Bank downtown when he died."

"So?"

She groaned. "Oh, come on, Bruce. You know what kind of people own it. You can't ignore that connection."

"Decatur Bank employs thousands of people nationally. Just because someone worked there—"

"It's my intuition, alright?" Valance snapped.

For a second, Bannockburn looked like he was going to walk to his car and drive off without looking back, but then he said, "You do have pretty fucking good intuition. It doesn't follow the pattern of children, though." He sighed, and his shoulders softened. "But I guess there's a first for everything. I assume he was a human, right?"

Valance hesitated uncharacteristically. "Well, not quite. He's a shifter." Bannockburn groaned, but Valance jumped in with, "Vampires can turn shifters. Granted, all accounts say it would have to be either an Alpha or Beta vamp, but those exist. It could happen!"

The corporal stared down at his feet and kicked at a spec of dirt. "Nah, I don't feel good about this one, Valance. Sorry. Maybe vamps can turn shifters, but we don't have anything solid to make the case. I can't get behind this one."

Valance snarled, and Green took a quick step back. "You can't support it because you don't believe it or because you don't want to believe it. You don't think the prospect of vampires turning paranormals scares the shit out of me, too? But look at what's been happening. They've been snatching up kids, one of whom might've been a paranormal in the making. They're doing *something* with their blood to create, I don't know, a drug? Something that's making people explode. Who's to say they aren't engineering other things? These bloodsuckers have all the resources and all the power. They're capable of things we can't even imagine."

"Then let's not spend all our energy trying to imagine them," Bannockburn snapped.

Green took another half step back. Had anyone ever spoken that way to Valance? Bannockburn either knew something Green didn't, or he was out of his goddamn mind.

Or they're banging. No. Too much. He couldn't even consider it.

"Don't you think we have enough on our hands without making things up?" the corporal continued. "What you just said was one assumption on top of another. That's the kind of shit that will get you, and maybe even Green and me fired, and then what good are we?"

Valance puffed in and out through round nostrils but kept her jaw clenched and her lips pressed into a thin white line.

"I'm not calling this in as a vamp," Bannockburn concluded, frowning. "If you want to, that's up to you. I'm not gonna stop—"

She snatched the radio from her belt. "Fang 9-01 to Fang 9-90. We have a 10-87. Requesting supervisor backup."

Green and Bannockburn exchanged wide-eyed glances.

She'd done it. She'd really done it. Radioed in a vampire sighting where anyone could hear it.

"Oh shit," Green said without meaning to.

"Shit indeed," Valance said. "We're already knee-deep in it. Might as well stop pretending it's mud." She turned and headed inside again.

Green watched her go then looked back at the corporal, who grimaced and followed her inside, mumbling, "Guess we're doing this." Then, "Mic, Rookie."

"Oh shoot." Green fumbled with his cord and got the thing hooked up. Whether it was working was something else entirely. But he could claim technical ignorance on it, and no one was likely to argue.

"Mrs. Jackson," Valance said. "We believe your husband might be a vampire."

The woman's head swiveled around to look at the other officers before she laughed, her eyes still bloodshot. "I'm pretty sure I mentioned that my husband is ... was ... is a shifter. He can't be a vampire."

Green could tell it was taking all of Bannockburn's control to keep from jumping in, throwing Valance under the bus, and cleaning up this mess. "There is, theoretically, a slim chance he could still be a vampire."

The woman turned to Green. "What about you? You haven't said a word. Do you believe this bullshit, too?"

"Mrs. Jackson, I'm here to follow protocol, and the vampire protocol has been initiated."

The woman's shock turned to outrage. "I demand to speak to a supervisor!"

"He's on his way," Valance said. "I already called him in. We'll take care of this vamp, don't worry. You're not in any danger at the moment."

"If there *is* a vamp, he's my husband! You can't just shoot him!"

"Well, technically, you're only a few houses down from an elementary school, and the law says they can't be within two hundred yards, so."

"Officer Valance," Bannockburn squeezed out through gritted teeth. "You're not helping."

"*Fang 9-90 approaching the address of the 10-87,*" came Montoya's voice over their radios.

"I'll stay here with Mrs. Jackson," Bannockburn said. "You two go meet him."

Valance was willing to follow that order, at least, and as they stepped out onto the front lawn, Green keeping an eye out for a vampire that looked like Mr. Jackson, Montoya turned onto the lane, his lights flashing. He parked in the middle of the street, killed the engine but kept the lights on, got out, walked around to his trunk, and pulled out his nightstick. Valance and Green hadn't made it ten feet toward Montoya before a figure appeared, moving slowly out of the shadows toward the sergeant.

Valance pulled a retractable wooden stake from her belt, flicked her wrist to extend it and snap it firmly into place, and took two hurried steps forward before stopping in her tracks. "God ... fucking ... dammit."

As the zombie staggered forward, drawn toward the whirling lights, Montoya met it halfway, reared back, and swung his nightstick as hard as he could, sending the zombie's head flying off its shoulders. The rest of the body crumpled to the asphalt, and the head rolled to a stop just a few yards away from where Valance stood and continued to curse. She pressed the release button on her stake, retracted it again, and jammed it back into her duty belt.

"That your guy?" Montoya hollered over, pointing at the head on the ground.

Valance approached, kicked it with her boot to turn it until she could see the face. She scowled then kicked the head back into the road before stomping her way across the yard and down toward where the meth-head shifter must live.

"Fucking necromancers," she grumbled. And Green almost felt sorry for the suspect she was about to arrest.

———

Valance was silent and broody at show-up the next night, but that wasn't too shocking, considering the justified tongue lashing she'd received from Montoya the night before.

She leaned against the back wall of the meeting room—that part, at least, didn't deviate from her routine—sipping her black coffee and daring anyone, more so than usual, to look at her the wrong way.

That was a game Green wasn't keen to play, so instead, he sat toward the front of the room next to Brooks, who chatted away with Marrow about the backup weapons they had their eye on once the next paycheck rolled in the following day.

Montoya walked in, and the chatter died down. He cut right to the chase, smacking the projector until it turned on. The first slide was already queued up. "Anna Pfaff." He flipped to the next slide. "Caitlin Holloway. Still no sign of them, and while we're on week two for Holloway and three for Pfaff, we're not calling this case closed until we at least find their bodies. Unfortunately, we're pretty sure that's all we'll find. Two young girls were taken from the same wealthy neighborhood. Likely, we have another psychopath on our hands. One more disappearance and the Bureau is likely to be called in and classify this as the work of a serial killer. Nothing we can do about that; just wanted to give a heads up."

"Sir," Officer Brooks said, "I have a friend who works for the Bureau, and from what she's told me, this doesn't follow the pattern of a typical serial killer."

Montoya held up a hand to silence her. "I'm sure we'll get plenty of opinions from them soon as they swoop down on us. If it's all the same to you, I'll wait until then before subjecting myself to their theories. In the meantime, we have other concerns. Like Marcus Franchioni." He flipped to the next slide. "Stabbed his brother twenty-seven times last night and then fled the scene. Shouldn't be far or particularly hard to find. He has a sweet tooth for PCP, so odds are, he'll do something stupid and hard to miss before long. And when he does, he'll be naked and ready to do battle. But he also comes from a prestigious werewolf family out of Emerald Hills, so if we could please not shoot the asshole, that would be fantastic. Tasers, okay?"

"And if he shifts?" Marrow asked. "We supposed to try to tase a wolf on PCP, or should we just forget about the tasing completely and try to hump him into submission?"

Montoya wasn't amused, though most of the shift was. "Fine. You have advance permission to shift if needed to neutralize the situation."

"What about Green?" asked Lawrence. "What's he supposed to do if he can't shift?"

Montoya's round shoulders stiffened, his agitation no longer contained to his voice. "Call in backup that can shift!

Shit, you people know how to do your job without getting killed, right?"

"Sure," Harmon said, "but my guns are a big part of that."

"Goddammit! Fine. Shoot the werewolf!" Montoya shouted, his face a tomato. "Let's have us a goddamn species riot! And while we're at it, let's align ourselves with the side that doesn't have any of the money or resources! Why the hell not?"

Green glanced at Patrick Harmon a few rows back, where the long-time patrol officer failed to suppress a stupid grin at having been the one to push Montoya over the edge this time around. Then Green's eyes landed on Valance and Bannockburn where they leaned against the wall next to one another. From the proximity and casual body language of the two, she didn't appear too upset with her corporal about what had gone down the night before.

Bannockburn leaned over and whispered something in Valance's ear that made a small grin twitch at the corner of her lips.

Oh, shit. They *were* banging. They had to be.

"I almost forgot to mention," Montoya continued at the front of the meeting room, "that your shift has earned itself a special assignment. You're each to come in two hours before the end of tonight's shift to endure—and I choose that word intentionally—a department-led sensitivity training."

"Oh, for fuck's sake!" Brooks shouted ahead of the torrent of cursing that rose up from the small group.

Lawrence stood from his chair. "Just because Valance won't stop whipping her dick out and calling in 10-87s, we *all* have to sit through two hours of horseshit?"

"No," Montoya said, a tiny victorious grin spreading on his red face. "Not *everyone* has to attend." He paused as things started to settle down. "All of *you* have to, but I don't."

As the gripes began anew, Montoya shouted over the ruckus, "It's not just the Fang 900s. There'll be individuals from other shifts. So, I better not find out about you insensitive assholes making a scene, you hear?" No one replied in the affirmative, but apparently that wasn't required. "Whatever." Montoya motioned for them to stand and move toward the door. "Get the hell out of here and try not to shoot anybody."

———

After seeing the friendliness between Valance and Bannockburn, and still unable to accept that the two might be kissing cousins, Green wondered it Valance wasn't as upset about the previous night's reprimand as he'd initially suspected. If she wasn't mad at Bannockburn, who was her superior and had openly sided with Montoya after the call, there was no reason why she would be mad at Green. Not after he'd her back and stuck to consoling Mrs. Jackson about her decapitated husband, not only because someone needed to, but to stay out of the politics as much as possible. Sometimes being a rookie and having everyone expect you to blindly take the orders of your superiors without holding you at all accountable for said orders could be a blessing.

As Valance loaded up her trunk, speaking in low tones with Bannockburn, who stood less than a foot away, Green approached. The corporal caught sight of him first, nodded, and then headed off to his own car. Valance turned a bored expression on Green. "You need something?"

"I just wanted to check on you. Make sure everything's okay?"

She chuckled. "Aw, that's cute. You still think 'okay' is an achievable state." Her humor faded rapidly. "If you're wondering whether my career is on the chopping block, no, it's not. I've weathered worse shitstorms, and I'll weather this one. If you're wondering whether I want to make a buffalo skin throw rug out of Montoya, yeah, I do. But all good things come in due time."

"Have you given up on the whole, you know, search for the V-word?" He mumbled the last sentence, hoping she hadn't already activated her body mic.

She stared scornfully at him. "Who are you, Knox? No, I gave up on that a long time ago. I mean, I went through a phase while I was in Guatemala but—" She stopped herself. "Oh, you mean vampires. No, I haven't given up on that. That's a stupid thing to give up on. Especially when Montoya made it so obvious how hellbent he is on keeping me from finding one." She leaned close. "You notice how quickly he made it to the address when I called in a 10-87? You ever known him to haul ass anywhere?" She grinned, her thin lips curling back to show a glimmer of her straight, ivory teeth. "We both know he was back at the sub, sitting on his ass when that call came out. He must've flown down the highway." She cackled. "Man! What I wouldn't pay to hear the things coming out of his mouth as he drove. The fact that I'm not cursed at this moment is proof that Montoya doesn't have an ounce of real magic in him, no matter what he insists about his ancestors."

Watching Valance in such a state of vengeful jubilance

was like watching a volcano shoot lava two hundred feet into the air—powerful, unbelievable, maybe even beautiful, but what went up had to come down, and when it did …

Green decided to get a move on. "Okay, well, um, I'm glad you're not fired." He turned to walk away, but Valance hollered after him, her tone controlled once again. "Rookie."

He glanced cautiously over his shoulder.

"Thanks for coming when I said the word. Good to know I have someone who'll watch my back."

"Uh, sure thing."

"Or, at least *try* to watch my back. Just as likely you get killed in the process."

Green narrowed his eyes at his former FTO. "Why are you like this?"

She shook her head minutely. "I don't know what you mean."

He waved her off and headed to his car.

As frustrating and, frankly, baffling as he found it, Green had Valance's back, and he would continue to have it, just like he knew she would have his.

Heather Valance is going to be the death of me.

CHAPTER ELEVEN

The shift was a brutal one, but sometimes that happened for no discernible reason. It wasn't a full moon. It wasn't a weekend. It was just a damn Tuesday. A Tuesday where everyone in Fang sector lost their mind. Green was quickly learning that there was no rhyme or reason to why everyone seemed to lose their goddamn mind all in one night, only that it happened, and when it did, it was best not to think too hard about it.

Even with the shift being cut short by two hours, Green felt like he'd just worked twenty-four straight. And as the rest of the Fang 900s shuffled into the classroom at the academy for their mandatory sensitivity training, it was clear Green wasn't alone in having been put through the wringer.

"Is it possible," Brooks said as she flopped down into a seat next to her work wife, Marrow, a row ahead of Green, "that sometimes things just spontaneously combust? Because it sure as hell feels like there are not enough pyromancers in this entire city to account for all the goddamn fires I saw tonight."

Marrow sighed but didn't reply, so Brooks continued. "I passed two dumpster fires on my way to a car fire. And then I got to the car fire and had to leave it because there was a bigger house fire right down the block!"

With a loud whoosh of air from his lungs, Harmon dropped his ass into a chair next to Green and turned toward the women. "Get this. I was trying to pull over a drunk driver who was swerving all over the highway. He turns the wrong way onto a one-way street to evade, crashes his car into a fire hydrant, which he knocks loose, then all the water is shooting everywhere, and *still* his car bursts into flames. Then he jumps out, on fire, and breaks into *another* vehicle, tries to drive away, but of course *that* car catches on fire from his fire, so he bails out, shifts into, I dunno, an eagle or something? It looks more like a phoenix because the idiot is still flaming. He dive-bombs an old tree and sets *that* on fire. So now the whole block is up in flames, and I'm like, well heck if I can do anything about this. I call Fire and tell them to pause whatever video game they'd been playing all night and get their lazy bums out to the scene."

Brooks nodded sympathetically. "Did the suspect blow above the legal limit?"

Harmon shrugged a single shoulder, presumably all he could muster. "Beats me. That guy is *super* dead. Shouldn't have changed into a bird when he was on fire."

A body flopped down on the other side of Green, and when he turned to see who it was, he was surprised by the sight of Agent Saffron from SHU next to him. She flashed him an extra-toothy grin then leaned across him toward

Harmon. "Can you believe this, Patrick? I exorcised three demons tonight—three!—one of whom claimed to be Satan himself, although that's not uncommon with these tiny-pricked entities. And I had to wrap up early on a night like tonight and head to sensitivity training! You're the most culturally sensitive person I know, and they got you in here, too!"

Harmon bobbed his head and rolled his eyes. "Are you actually surprised? It's been almost an entire year since we were both in here, listening to the same dumb lectures."

"True," said Agent Saffron. "Maybe there are some new and improved techniques for being sensitive to demons and their feelings that I can glean from this. Oh no! Do you think they've just been horribly misunderstood this whole time? Maybe rather than banishing them, I should have asked them about their mothers." She rolled her eyes and leaned back in her seat, grabbing her canvas bag from the floor by her chair and setting it onto her lap before yanking it open, rifling around in it, and pulling out a small, glass vial of turquoise powder. She popped open the cork stopper, dipped a long fingernail in, scooping up a small amount, then lifted it to her nostril and inhaled deeply until the powder was gone.

Green leaned away quickly and whipped his head around toward Harmon, mouthing, "What was that?"

Harmon shut his eyes gently and, with a small wave of his hand, indicated that Green should let it go.

Valance strolled in, appearing in better spirits than the rest of the attendees. Bannockburn entered only a step behind.

"Fancy them arriving together," Marrow whispered to Brooks.

Valance and Bannockburn slid into a row behind Marrow and Brooks, and before long, the whole shift was there, plus others who had been assigned sensitivity training on an individual basis, like Agent Saffron and a few other officers Green recognized from brief interactions as they worked overtime for the Fang 900s or chatted in jail. None he particularly wanted to chat with again, though, and as he looked around, he realized that, yeah, pretty much everyone deserved to be here except maybe a few from his shift. He included himself in that exception.

"O-kay," announced an unfamiliar and nasally male voice a second before a man in black slacks, a white button-down, and a charcoal gray trench coat sauntered into the classroom. He was followed closely by a similarly dressed man a foot taller than anyone else in the room. "I'm Detective Ney, and this is Detective Kidd. We're here to teach you jackholes how to stop making your life harder on the job."

They hadn't brought anything along with them that Green could see, which boded well. No dumb activities, no visual aids. Maybe this would wrap up early, and he could go home, shower a couple of times, and pass out for a good four hours before he had to wake up and do it all again.

At the front of the room, Detective Ney leaned his butt against a heavy wooden table, crossing his arms over his chest and his feet at the ankles. He lacked the local accent, laying it on thick with a northeastern one Green had always associated with people whose impulse control was only slightly better than a rabid possum's. "Here's the deal. You're here because you're not perfect at your job. In fact, some of you probably suck at your job. We're gonna make you more sensitive whether you like it or not."

"That's a promise," said Detective Kidd in a deep vibrato. He stood behind the table, looming over Ney's shoulder and serving little clear purpose so far other than to stare intimidatingly at the unfortunate souls in the audience of this mandatory lecture.

"We know what each of you did." He moved two fingers between his eyes and the eyes of Officer Grey of the Alpha 700s, and Green was instantly ravenous to know what the hell Grey had done to get himself thrown in here with the rest of the degenerates.

But then Detective Ney scanned the room and did the same thing to Officer Valance, which seemed unwise for a lot of reasons. Valance met his glare and then did the finger thing right back at him.

"Heard some of you been going on a witch hunt out there—"

Agent Saffron raised a finger into the air. "I find that term offensive to my people."

"I find you talking outta turn offensive!" Ney snapped, and when he turned his attention to the other side of the room, doing the finger thing to Officer Lee from the Banshee 800s, Green leaned forward to Brooks and whispered, "Is this guy on drugs?"

She nodded slowly but firmly. "Narcotics detective."

"But that doesn't mean—"

"Rookie!" Ney hollered. "You got something you want to share with the class? Whispering while I'm up here putting myself out there in front of all you sons of bitches—"

"I find that term sexist," Valance called from the back.

Ney jabbed a finger sharply toward her. "I'll get to you later, missy." He turned to Green, picking up where he left off. "I'm up here, putting myself in front of all you sons and daughters of bitches, being vulnerable and whatnot, so how do you think it makes me feel when you go whispering like that? I'll tell you. It makes me feel sad in my emotions!" He clutched his heart, twisting up his face like he was passing a kidney stone as he stared at Green, who had frozen, his ass hovering above his chair as he leaned near Brooks, the second Ney had rounded on him.

Detective Ney turned to the rest of the class, his arms spread wide, a squinty grin on his face. "See? You see what I did there? I just taught that dirt-for-brains rookie what it feels like when he does insensitive things. And over the next two hours, Detective Kidd and I will do that to each of you." He curled his lips back in a fierce snarl as he jabbed a finger at each person in the class. "Yeah, each and every one of yas."

Green finally plopped back into his seat, and Harmon said, "You get used to it. The guys leading it last year brought in some of the people we arrested *that night* and made us listen to how arresting them in front of their families made them feel."

"Jesus," Green whispered.

"What'd I *just* say about whispering?" Ney whined, his eyes opening wide, one significantly more than the other.

"Sorry, sir."

Ney shoved his sleeves further up his tan forearms. "Okay, now let's talk about what it means to be sensitive. It means," he held up a hand and listed it off on his fingers, "bein' inclusive! That means you don't tell the rookie he's retarded just because he's human."

Green looked around at his shift mates. Did they think that about him?

"It means you listen; ya hear that, Rookie? It means you

shut your mouth for a fucking second and listen when I tell you your whispering makes me feel yucky in my emotions!"

Oh, God. Was this hazing? Could this be an elaborate practical joke? Just in case it wasn't, Green steadied his expression and nodded sympathetically.

"It also means that when a woman is grieving the loss of her husband, you don't go telling her he's been turned into a damn vamp when in reality he's just been necro-ed into a zombie!" He glared at Valance, jabbing the three counting fingers at her like a trident. "And *sometimes* it means that you don't tell a pretty lady that she's hot and you're down to clown because maybe she's a dyke and doesn't appreciate your flawless male anatomy." He cleared his throat. "You wise guys ... and gals got anything to say for yourselves?"

No one did.

"That's right. Ya ain't got no defense for your actions. So, let's start with inclusion." He stepped to the side. "Detective Kidd?"

Kidd lumbered over to a small lectern, reached into his coat pocket and pulled out a stack of note cards. He cleared his throat, then, in a voice so deep Green could hardly understand the words, began reading off them. "The Statute of Non-Discrimination and Equal Workplace Safety and Security consists of five primary tenets. Section one covers discrimination based upon species, subspecies, sex, gender, race, religion and creed, but is not limited to ..."

At the end of an eight-hour shift that had left Green not sure whether he should wash with soap and water or hydrochloric acid and lighter fluid, Detective Kidd's part of the training was markedly worse than Ney's pugilistic seminar.

After an hour and fifty-two minutes of intense struggle

to remain awake and without learning a single thing about sensitivity, Green was finally spared the battle against sleep when Ney started shouting again. "What I'm seeing is a bunch of cops who need to go home and get some sleep. See? That's me being observant and sensitive to your needs. You fucktards could use a little bit of that out on the streets. And because I'm such a nice, sensitive guy, I'm gonna let you out early."

Green glanced at his watch. It was thirty seconds before the scheduled release time.

"But first, I need each of you to scribble your name on this paper that's going around, saying you were here and one thing you learned. Then you can go."

The sign-up sheet started on the opposite side of the room.

There went the early release.

Harmon rubbed a hand down his face, causing his bottom lip to flap back audibly against his teeth. "You owe us donuts tomorrow, Valance."

"Screw that," Lawrence said. "Kolaches. This *might* have been a donut-level offense if we'd gotten a trained instructor. But Ney and Kidd are certifiably insane. Maybe criminally so. That bumps this up to a kolache offense. And not just any kolaches, but the ones from Baba's. Pork, beef, bacon—the works."

The rest of the shift nodded, and the verdict was officially passed.

"Fine," said Valance. "But only because it's between my home and the substation."

Green stopped his tired brain from blurting, "You have a home?" While it seemed obvious that she did once he thought about it, he'd never thought about it. But of course.

Valance wasn't working all the time. What exactly did she do in her free hours?

His eyes jumped over to Bannockburn as if giving his brain a not-so-subtle hint.

Valance snatched the clipboard from Agent Saffron before it made it through the rest of the shift. After scribbling her name and one thing she'd learned, she passed it to Bannockburn who did the same then shoved it at Green, before following Valance out of the classroom.

Green watched them leave together and then stared down at the clipboard, looking for the next open line. Instead, his attention went to Valance's surprisingly legible handwriting and the one thing she learned: *If I snort enough blow, I can one day lead sensitivity training.*

Then below that, next to Bannockburn's name: *If you sexually harass a woman long enough, and assuming she's not a lesbian, you can get in her pants.*

Green's head jerked around toward the exit, but Bannockburn and Valance were already long gone. "They *are* boning," he whispered.

"Yeah, no shit," Agent Saffron said before gathering her things and waddling out of the row toward the door.

"If I didn't know any better," Marrow said, "I'd guess you were jealous, Green."

"What? No."

"Yeah," she persisted, "you took forever to accept it because you want to be the one trapped in the death grip of her thighs. Seriously, I've heard stories. She's killed men with them."

Lawrence inserted a hand between Marrow and Green. "Firstly, that's insensitive to Green's basic male needs. Every man in this room has thought about boning every woman in this room, and either because of our better judgment or because we couldn't make the cut, we didn't." He paused, staring at the far wall, then quickly added, "Or we did, and it didn't work out." Green scanned the faces of his shift mates to get a read on that, but they all seemed just as confused.

Except for Brooks, who was suddenly interested in the ceiling tiles.

"The main thing I'm getting at," Lawrence continued, addressing Marrow, Harmon, and Brooks, "is that I've already discussed this with Green, and he's not interested. Right?" Lawrence looked at him.

"Right."

"You gotta admit, though," Marrow said, snatching the clipboard from Green, who wasn't doing anything with it, "it would explain why you follow her around and do basically everything she tells you to."

"Lay off," Brooks said. "He's still a rookie. She was his FTO. He's gonna have a little hero worship for a while until he gets more experience under his belt."

"Is that why Lawrence followed you around after you were his FTO?" Marrow asked, grinning mischievously.

"Yes," Lawrence and Brooks said quickly.

"I'm right here," Green said. "Stop talking about me like I'm not."

Brooks turned farther in her seat to rest a hand on his shoulder. "We just worry about you. This stuff with vampires that Valance is all hung up on? It's the same old shit she always does."

Harmon nodded. "Dark Lord knows we all fell for it at one point or another. You're just new, and you've already narrowly avoided the department hanging you out to dry once. I, for one, don't want to see you taken down by her conspiracies."

"Um, thanks, Harmon."

The clipboard made its rounds, and this time Green was the last to get it. The rest of his shift had cleared off when Lawrence handed it over to him and said, "Go get some sleep or meet a nice, willing lady or something. You deserve it." He winked.

Green nodded, scribbled his name on the first open line, then wrote: *Whispering is a trigger for Detective Ney.* He clicked his pen, shoved it back in his breast pocket, tossed the clipboard onto the table by which Ney and Kidd stood, deep in conversation. Then he sprinted out of the classroom before either of the detectives could read the list.

CHAPTER TWELVE

Officer Marrow led the way with Green a few steps behind as they approached the property mentioned in the burglery call. She'd graciously drawn her gun, allowing him to go with less lethal force in the form of a beanbag shotgun from his trunk.

While the caller had remained anonymous, Green had run the info on the address to discover that the last known resident, according to Kilhaven Utilities, was Chester Michaels. Further searches turned up that he had a wife and two kids.

And also, that he was a cherub.

It was that last detail that bumped the call up to a high priority. Tara Marrow and Norman Green were less than two minutes away when the call went up on his HAM, and he assigned—mostly because it was the right thing to do, but also because he hoped to get a glimpse of a young cherub in the flesh. He'd heard they were about as adorable as adorable came.

Not that he would ever admit that motivation to his fellow officers and not that it remained his primary motivation as he approached the lush, green yard of the Michaels house.

The landscaping looked out of place in the generally low-income immigrant neighborhood with four-foot chain-link fences surrounding each front yard as well as the back. The houses on either side seemed much less concerned with the greenery, one opting for the aesthetic of rusty scrap metal while the other went with the classic dying palm tree and brown grass look.

When a house in Fang sector had this much greenery surrounding it, that meant one of three things: it was occupied by cherubim, who had a particular affinity for gardening, it was occupied by criminals, who didn't want the cops to have an easy line of sight to shoot into the windows, or it was occupied by criminal cherubim.

The streetlight in front of the Michaels' home was out. He paused before passing underneath when he spotted the large pieces of the covering, not yet run over by tires, indicating that this had probably been a recent development and an intentional modification. Probably shot out, perhaps by whoever had entered the home.

Green whispered for Marrow to stop, then he indicated the broken pieces of the cover and explained his theory to Marrow. She nodded.

He was especially proud of his observation and struggled not to think of how he might employ the mention of it to his benefit the next time he found himself alone at a bar.

Green and Marrow approached in the cover of darkness. The gate squeaked unhelpfully as they slid beyond it, and

Green was forced to give up one of his hands to push away overgrown vines and branches that reached across the walkway up to the front porch steps.

The lights in the house were off and the porch light, too, was shattered.

"Should we wait for backup?" Green asked as they paused at the top of the three steps, just underneath the awning.

"Caller said she heard moaning coming from inside. Lights are broken. You think we have time to wait for more backup?"

A similar situation kept rattling around in his head, and he half expected there to be a man carving off and eating chunks of a woman's leg just beyond the front door. But as much anxiety as that image stirred in him, the prospect of calling in the Telekinetics Unit stirred even more.

Please don't make me call TU. He shut his eyes, sending his message out to God, the Universe, Dracula, or whoever else might listen.

"Fang 9-14 requesting backup. Going in with 9-07. Requesting backup." She took her finger off the radio on her shoulder and looked at him. "There. You ready?"

He nodded, and Marrow grabbed the handle. It turned.

The door swung open.

Green and Marrow stood on either side listening, but they heard nothing.

"Kilhaven Police," Green announced.

Still nothing.

"We're coming in," Marrow shouted. "We're just here to check up on you."

Marrow was short enough that when she went in first,

Green was able to see clear over her head, which had its tactical benefits. When the tac light on Marrow's gun wasn't enough to make him feel safe in the pitch-black house, he clicked on his flashlight, careful not to backlight her, offering up her silhouette like a sacrifice to whoever might lay in wait, hoping to ambush a couple of cops.

Because that was what this had to be. An ambush. It didn't make sense any other way. And yet, they still had to walk into it.

The Kilhaven Police recruiters had included a thorough job description on the brochure they handed him at that college job fair, but walking into traps over and over again, for some strange reason, had been omitted.

Not too late to be a janitor. I bet people only ambush them with oddly placed turds.

Had it not been for the broken lights and the unlocked front door, Green might have been happy concluding that the Michaelses were on a family vacation somewhere and this was all a silly mix-up caused by a busybody neighbor who overheard a stray cat giving birth.

But this didn't add up. Something more nefarious was at play; Green just didn't know what yet. He felt certain he'd find out before long, and probably in a painful way.

They passed the kitchen on their right, a narrow staircase on their left as they headed into the back of the house, presumably toward the living room, since they hadn't encountered anything that could pass as one yet.

But it wasn't until they'd left the kitchen behind that Green started to hear a distinct dripping sound that reminded him of his first apartment, back when he was still in the academy and couldn't afford much more than a hovel.

The roof had leaked there, and because the landlord would be damned if he put a cent into upkeep, Green had resorted to placing a metal bucket beneath the leak every time it rained. The *drip, drip, drip* was still fresh in his mind months after leaving that shitheap behind.

And now he heard it again. There was a second story to this house, so if there was dripping, it meant one of two things.

They entered the living room, and when Green's flashlight beam fell upon the source of the tinny noise, he realized it hadn't indicated *either* of the two things he expected.

No, only a psychopath could anticipate something like this.

He jumped back the moment the scene finished its journey from his eyes to his brain, and he narrowly prevented himself from discharging his beanbag gun out of fear. "Oh, holy fuck!"

Marrow whirled around and took a few hurried steps away, too, before putting her back to the grotesque wall decoration and making quick work of clearing the rest of the living room.

Green tore his gaze from the splayed, bleeding body on the wall to help secure the rest of the floor.

He paused at the bottom of the staircase next to Marrow. The veteran was clearly frazzled herself, but she led the way up despite it.

One bedroom clear, then two, then three plus a bathroom. Whoever had done the heinous act downstairs appeared to be gone.

By the time they returned to the living room, the sickening dripping sound had slowed. Green hurried over to where the cherub was nailed upside down, adorable throat slit above a metal bucket that sat on the floor below, his wings spread out behind him. Thick nails through the wings, hands, and feet held the victim in place.

Green leaned his shotgun against the wall and leaned forward, checking for a pulse that he already knew wouldn't be there.

"Fang 9-07. We need a supervisor right away. Body found, undeniable signs of foul play."

Marrow kept an eye on the doorway, which led out of the living room and made a direct path to the front door. Though she kept it aimed at the ground, her firearm remained clutched in her hands.

"Vic is a male cherub, approximately"—he shined the flashlight on the victim's face and tilted to the side to get a better look, but no amount of light would help him guess a cherub's age—"adult. I think it's an adult. Probably Chester. No sign of his family."

"Fang 9-80 to 9-07," came Bannockburn's reply, and Green felt a few of the tight cords inside him slacken at hearing someone, especially Bannockburn, reply to the SOS. "Did you say cherub and foul play?"

"9-07. Yes, sir."

"Over on Orchid Brook? The suspicious sounds call?"

"Yes, sir. Need Homicide and a supervisor over here right away."

"9-80. Two blocks out. Start roping it off. Elves will be heading that way right behind me, I'm sure."

———

Bannockburn was right about the elves, and they arrived even before homicide made its way to the scene. It was a healthy reminder that the media was always watching and listening, which was fair enough for the sake of public accountability. But Green still wished the tall, lithe reporters in their thick-rimmed glasses and skinny jeans would give him and the rest of his colleagues some space to do their jobs.

Chester's brother Gino was called to the scene and showed Green a picture of Chester. It was definitely the man-baby inside, but until the detectives and medical examiner could be bothered to drag their ass to the scene and take care of their part of the process, no official identification could be made.

Gino fluttered nervously, feet a yard off the ground so he was at chest height with Bannockburn just inside the police line, out of earshot of the elves, as Green returned inside to brief Sergeant Montoya.

Two large semicircles of dark sweat were visible underneath the were-bison's armpits, even in the dim light, as Green approached the sergeant. The electric lanterns set around the remarkably average living room created a shrine-like feel, like the dead and bloodless body sat upon some pagan altar, a sacrifice to the monogod. "I called in Organized Crime, too," said Montoya. "The cherubim have been involved in too many calls lately, and I think something's up. OC seemed to think so, too, and they've asked to be kept up-to-date about any incidents involving cherubim, leprechauns or any other known gangs." He turned again toward the cupid on the wall. "Damn, I wish homicide would hurry up. Can't stand to keep looking at the little guy up there." He put a hand on Green's back. "Let's get out of here. You can get to work on your report, and I'll pull Marrow for the brief." He patted Green between the shoulder blades as they exited the house and entered onto the front porch where the air felt like a thick sludge and small slivers of red and blue lights cut through the dense and obscuring foliage. "You did well, Rookie. You've *done* well. Just in general. Keep your nose clean, and you got a long, lucrative career in this department." When Green turned to face him, searching for tells of sarcasm (and finding none), Montoya added, "I've seen a lot of rookies in my nineteen years on the Force, and I know when I see one that'll last and rise in the ranks. You're one. So, as I said,"—his eyebrows climbed his short forehead—"keep your nose clean, and you got a bright future ahead of you."

Green heard the real message loud and clear. "Yes, sir." But whether he intended to follow the advice was a different thing entirely.

Bannockburn was finishing up with Gino just outside the fence when Montoya opened the gate and stepped aside for Green to go first.

"Corporal," Montoya said. "You've dealt with this sort of thing plenty. Will you make sure Green knows the procedure going forward while I have a word with Mr. Michaels here?"

Bannockburn nodded respectfully. "Too much media out here. We'll talk in your car." Green agreed, and when he slipped into the driver's side, Bannockburn was already seated in the passenger's side. "Take a quick lap around the block to get your head on straight, Rookie."

"Huh?"

"Trust me."

Green started up his car, and once he'd rounded the

corner, Bannockburn went to work, disabling the dash cam, unplugging the HAM, then his body mic, then Green's body mic. Bannockburn's sudden contact with Green's chest caused him to swerve slightly, as he realized how long it'd been since anyone besides those resisting arrest had touched him.

"Cherubim are ready to talk," the corporal said.

"Great. Organized Crime will be happy to—"

"Not to those ass clowns. You know why they're called Organized Crime? Because they're the most organized criminals in this goddamn town. And they'll stay that way until leadership gets its head out of its ass and decides to stop ignoring the problem, hoping it goes away."

"No, the cherubim are ready to talk to *me*," finished Bannockburn.

"To you? Why you?"

"Because the name Bannockburn still means something in this town. The enemy of my enemy is my friend."

"But the cherubim enemies are the leprechauns. Do leprechauns and timberweres get along, or—?"

"We get along fine. You're thinking about it in the wrong direction, Green."

"What direction should I be thinking about it in, then?"

"If the cherubim want to solicit the help of the weres, they're assuming we would want to help. The only reason they would assume that is if their perceived enemy was also *our* enemy. And who's our enemy, Green?"

It was starting to make sense, but there were still so many missing links between the thoughts. "Va—" Then he remembered what Valance had told him about mentioning that word, especially around Bannockburn. He didn't want to blow the corporal's cover.

"It's alright. You can say it."

"Valance told me not to."

"She's not here."

Green hesitated, and Bannockburn sighed. "This isn't some convoluted test, Rookie. She says no, I say yes, who do you choose? It's nothing like that. I disabled all the devices. Just say the damn word."

"Vampires."

"There you go. And you're right."

"You think the cherubim are dealing with vampires? You think a vampire did that to Chester Michaels?"

"Pfft. Hell no. Vampires like to keep their talons clean. The blunt force trauma to the vic's skull was a dead giveaway as to who the vamps have working at their behest."

Now it made sense. Sort of. "Why would the leprechauns do the vampires' dirty work?"

Bannockburn sighed and rolled his neck in circles, stretching it out after a long shift. "That's the question. I expect we'll know a lot more once the cherubim start talking. I'll pass it along to Valance, and she'll fill you in, understand?"

"Got it."

Bannockburn went to work reconnecting the equipment, and once he was done and they were back where they started in front of the scene, he said, "You got some truly bad luck with electronics, Rookie. If I didn't know any better, I'd say you pissed off the wrong leprechaun." He nodded and left Green alone to digest that last statement. Could leprechauns cast curses? What the hell? He swore at himself for not paying better attention in the academy.

Being a C-student didn't cut it in some situations, he supposed.

Well, if this cherubim-leprechaun-vampire clusterfuck kept going the way it was, it wouldn't be long before Green found out all kinds of new things about leprechauns. And, as usual, he'd learn it all the hard way.

CHAPTER THIRTEEN_

Green knew he only had a few minutes of hot water left in this shower, and he was determined to use every drop of it. The complex charged a set amount for utilities every month, one that Green knew to be way overpriced, so he did his best not to let those slumlords make a quick buck off of him.

When he'd moved from the hovel where he'd spent months during the academy to his new apartment, he considered it a massive upgrade. But it didn't take long for all the cut corners around his new place to rear their ugly heads, and now he couldn't wait until his pay increased, and his overtime money went farther, and he could get the hell out. Maybe he'd move to the suburbs.

But no, he'd never find a girlfriend in the suburbs. Not if he couldn't find a decent one in the city. There were women everywhere in Kilhaven, but thanks to long hours, his interactions with them were limited to inherently unromantic situations. Maria Cortes had been something else, for instance. He'd met her two nights previous on one of his calls. Had they met in a bar, he was pretty sure his advances wouldn't be turned down. But as it was, their small talk consisted mostly of him explaining the cycle of abuse to her, informing her she was neck deep in it, and adding, as tenderly as he could, that her boyfriend would eventually kill her if she didn't leave.

He was desperate, but not hit-on-a-domestic-violence-victim desperate. Jesus.

Nothing to do but jerk off again, I guess.

It'd have to be quick or else it wouldn't work. The impending loss of hot water was like a ticking clock, so he went to it, swatting away his circular thoughts as they surfaced one-by-one.

No dead babies. You don't have to think about that now.

Shit! No, don't think about vampires, either.

This was a losing battle, and part of him knew it. The suspense Corporal had left him with two days before about the leprechaun–vampire connection was enough to drive him mad.

I wonder if leprechauns have a special way of fucking?

He considered it, even tried to stir up a visual, but it didn't help him move closer toward his goal.

Was it too much to ask for a man to enjoy the simple and goodly pleasure of a spank session?

How did others working patrol manage a love life?

The answer came to him immediately, like his brain was just waiting for him to ask the question.

They bone other officers.

Was that why Valance and Bannockburn were hooking up? Out of convenience? He couldn't exactly blame them. A warm body was worth every second of hell one might have to endure later. Even if it was Valance's warm body. And Valance's hell.

No, especially if it's Valance's.

That almost worked. Conjuring an image of her appearing at his doorstep dressed in street clothes, tendrils of her espresso hair falling over her shoulders...

He needed it so badly; he didn't care what line he crossed. Not anymore.

But not even a second after his climax, the terror swept in like the angel of death.

"No. Nooo! I can't. This can't become a thing. Oh God, if she ever finds out this was a thing ..."

The hot water ran out in a blink, but that was fine. He deserved every droplet of the frigid spray as he washed himself off.

Once he finished, he shut off the water with a frantic twist of his wrist, jumped out of the shower, wrapping a towel around his lower half, and hurried away from the scene of the crime.

Just as the elastic waistband of his briefs snapped against his skin, concealing the smoking gun of his verboten activity, a loud knock at his front door caused his heart to jump into his throat.

Shit. What day was it? Was rent overdue?

But no, he'd paid last week.

Whoever this was, they brought ill tidings; Green was certain of that. Good news never showed up unannounced; only bad news did that.

After slipping on some gym shorts, he headed through his apartment, padding over the tan shag carpet to the front door. As any good officer would, he avoided the peephole, stepped to the side of the frame, and cracked open the door.

And like any properly shamed young boy might, he gasped when he saw who was standing there.

Had his jerking off somehow conjured her?

Of course not. That wasn't a thing.

Pull it together. She doesn't need to know. It was an accident. Nobody can prove anything! You can't be held responsible!

Valance wore street clothes and her hair loose around her shoulders just like he'd imagined her moments before.

"If you're worried about me seeing you in only your panties, don't worry. I've seen men disemboweled, so it won't be the most horrifying sight I've laid eyes on."

When he opened the door wider, her gaze traveled down him, taking in his bare chest, then further. "Did I come at a bad time?" she asked, staring at the small tent of his gym shorts.

"What? No. Just, uh ..."

She pushed past him with a duffle over her shoulder, and he wondered if she'd come to offer him more scent training. He sure as hell hoped not.

"Doesn't matter, Rookie. I'm happy for you if you can still get it up after that call the other night." She set the bag down on the coffee table and turned toward him. "I saw the crime scene photos. That was some hardcore shit."

"It's not— I'm not— Why are you here?" he asked, his hand on the open front door.

"Shut the door, and I'll tell you."

Against his better judgment, he did, closing himself inside with her. Then it occurred to him. "Bannockburn sent you." He walked over and stood on the opposite side of the coffee table, neither of them bothering to sit down.

"Sure did. It's as we suspected. Cherubim and leprechauns are in a drug war. Competing with each other for clients. The shooting at Eden was a warning for the cherubim to back off. Clearly, the leprechauns felt they had enough protection to try something that brash. Then Explodee McGee over at Feeney's happened, and leprechauns accused the cherubim of tampering with their supply. Been going back and forth since, ending with the murder of Chester Michaels who, by the way, has no mob affiliation. Gino, on the other hand." She rolled her eyes. "I guess they were sending a message or whatever. Anyway, cherubim don't turn a blind eye to the fucking obvious like old Chief Spinner or whoever else up top is suppressing this vamp scandal does. They noticed the purple, too. And the missing children. Rumor is, the Irish and the vamps have struck up some sort of symbiotic relationship."

"And that is?"

"God only knows. But it's enough to know you'll need this." She unzipped her bag and pulled out a silver chain with a pendant on the end, holding it out to him.

He grabbed it cautiously, but held it at arm's length, inspecting it. "What's this?"

"You're looking right at it, and you can't tell? Jesus. I could use shit like this to extort you so hard if you ever decide to try for detective."

He ignored her. "It's a gold coin."

"Bravo, Inspector. It's goddamn leprechaun gold. And yes, I stole it from evidence, so don't let anyone know you have it and *especially* don't let anyone know you got it from me. Odds are, it would've just sat in the locker until the sun swallows this sorry rock, so I've done everyone a favor and brought it back into circulation."

The coin might have been a circle at one point, but it was grossly misshapen now, and Green's guess at it being gold had been more a stereotype about coins than due to its actual appearance. It was mostly a brown color, and as he turned it over in his hand, he saw that each side bore a pressed image. Of what? God only knew. Far as he could tell, one side depicted week-old roadkill and the other a discarded diaper. "What am I supposed to do with this?"

"The chain didn't give you a hint?"

"Well, okay, sure. I'm supposed to wear it, but why?"

"They can't curse you while you're wearing it. And let me tell you, those sons of bitches curse people up and down. And getting them to lift a curse is the biggest pain in the ass. And usually, they stick you with vague things, like bad luck. Just sweeping shit like that." She chuckled dryly. "No, you don't want a leprechaun curse."

"Isn't that covered under assaulting a police officer?"

She nodded emphatically. "Oh, yeah. Super illegal to put a curse on a police officer. Definitely considered assault. Now tell me, Rookie, how many times have you been assaulted while on duty?"

He thought about it, counting in his head. "Five." Then, "Okay. I see your point." He slid the chain around his neck, cringing against the cold metal on his bare chest.

She zipped up her bag and threw it over her shoulder. "Bannockburn deserves the credit for that." She nodded at the chain. "He thought of it. I just swiped the coins."

"You two seem to spend a lot of time together lately."

"Yeah, I guess so. I mean, whenever we can."

"People have noticed it."

She tilted her head minutely, narrowing her eyes at him. "What do you mean?"

Why was he bringing this up? This was so not his business.

Unless their romance gets you found out and fired. Then it's definitely your business.

"The rest of the shift. They know what's going on between you and Corporal."

"No, they— Oh. You mean the fucking."

He took a quick step back, nearly choking on his saliva. "Shit, Valance."

"Well? That's what you were pussyfooting around, right?"

"I wasn't pussyfooting. Besides, don't you think it's a bad time for you and Bannockburn to be, you know ..."

"Destroying each other in bed?"

He stumbled back again, and his heels bumped up against his lopsided couch. "God. No. I mean, yes, but why did you have to say that?"

She shrugged.

"Shouldn't you two keep it in your pants until all this vamp stuff blows over?"

She frowned sympathetically, which Green knew better than to trust, and stepped around the table so she stood only a foot away from him. "I know. That's why we're not fucking, genius. But as long as people think we're disciplining each other in sexy and dangerous ways all day long, they'll chalk up our one-on-one time to *that* and overlook the fact that we're *uncovering a goddamn vampire conspiracy.*" She shook her head scornfully. "Come on, now, Rookie. You *know* what's going on here and you were still fooled."

"Don't you worry about Corporal getting in trouble for relations with an officer?"

"Maybe if we worked somewhere like Pan City, where the police leadership isn't a fucking cesspool, yes, but that's just a slap on the wrist in Kilhaven. They'll tell us we should have filled out paperwork, and then we'll fill out the paperwork, and they'll leave us alone. Nobody cares. Except you, it seems." She arched a brow at him and inched forward, her eyes falling to the coin resting on his bare skin. She placed her hand flat on it, pressing it to him, then to his horror and amazement, she traced her fingertips outward, over his heart, down his ribcage, over his abs, while he stood frozen.

When her fingertips were only an inch above the top of his shorts, she paused, staring up at his face through thick lashes. And when their eyes met, she tilted her head back, narrowing her eyes at him, and said, "Some buff mucker is going to tear you a new one if you don't bulk up. You're a walking target." She dropped her hand to her side and stepped back. "You know every substation has a gym, right? There's no excuse for you to be like you are."

She stepped around him and crossed the living room in half a dozen steps, pulling open the front door but pausing and turning to get one last look at him. "Also, if you eventually want to get laid by someone who's not a mushy taint, it wouldn't hurt to do a little strength training. As it is, someone like me would break you in two."

She winked and left, slamming the door behind her.

CHAPTER FOURTEEN

"Fang 9-01. We got us a dead one out in Twilight Delta trailer park. Poor sucker looks a few days expired."

Green paused as Valance's voice projected through the radio on his belt, echoing around the GasCo parking lot.

He'd spent an hour wringing info from the convenience store clerk who'd been sloppily robbed at gunpoint for a single pack of menthols. Green had never been a smoker, and if a nicotine addiction could cause people to pull shit like that, he was just fine staying away.

Having managed to avoid Valance all week since their mindfuck of an encounter at Green's apartment, code word or no code word, he wasn't looking to break his streak.

Besides, he had to finish this report, *and* it could be another false alarm. How many false alarms could go down with Valance, Green, and Bannockburn all on scene before it became blindingly obvious they were working together on this little extracurricular project?

So, he ignored it. That seemed like the best course of action for his career.

"You say somewhere between five-eight and six-three, maybe a hundred and fifty to three hundred pounds, had dark hair and his skin was tan, but maybe he was black?" Green looked up from his notes to the clerk to make sure he'd gotten it right.

"Yes, sir. I think he was a shifter, too."

"What makes you think that? You smell it on him?" It seemed unlikely, considering the victim was a human.

The clerk's eyes darted around. "He said, 'if anyone asks, I'm a shifter,' just before he ran out."

For shit's sake.

Green struggled to keep his eyes from rolling without his permission. *Robbery my ass.* Calls didn't get more bullshit than this.

"Okay, sir. Now, if you find that security footage that just happened to disappear, or you see this guy come back again, you call 911 right away. In the meantime, I'll submit this *detailed* report, and we'll make sure we can find the man who did this."

The clerk exhaled in a whoosh. "Thank you, Officer. I've always loved and respected law enforcement."

Oh, this guy is super guilty of something.

But Green didn't have the time or patience to stick around and figure out precisely what it was. Maybe the robbery was staged, but just as likely, the man was running around on his wife or has a half dozen trafficked virgins in the storage room. There was really no telling. And that was the way it went. Sometimes calls stank of lies, but there was no clear motive for the lying. Why did the clerk call the cops? He was going to lie, why wouldn't he say the suspect had stolen something worth more than a pack of cigarettes? There seemed no obvious explanation.

It reminded Green of the times growing up where he and his friends would get whiffs of shit, and, assuming someone had stepped on a dog turd, each checked their shoes only to find that everyone's were clean yet the phantom smell remained.

Looking back, one of his friends had probably shit his pants. Yeah, that made more sense.

As Green crawled into his vehicle and adjusted his duty belt, Corporal Bannockburn's voice piped up. "Fang 9-80. Just arrived on scene of the homicide. No immediate threat. We'll start questioning neighbors and keep the scene clear until homicide can come out. No rush. This sucker's not getting any deader."

"Fuck!" Green shouted. He pulled up the call on the HAM and assigned. "Fang 9-07 to Fang 9-80. Just finished up a call not far from Twilight Delta. Heading over to help secure the scene."

"9-80. Much appreciated. We'll get you in and outta here quick."

Much of the scene inside the trailer at Twilight Delta was as Green had expected it: a human victim lying bloodless on the floor, surrounded by general squalor.

What Green hadn't expected, though, was to find Brooks on scene. But she was there when he walked inside, and the shock of seeing her standing between Valance and Bannockburn, staring down at the body, caused Green to nearly step right into a puddle of crimson evidence as he entered.

"Watch it!" Bannockburn said, lurching forward, his hand out, eyes where Green's boot was about to land.

Green looked down and managed to divert his momentum just enough to slam his boot down to the side of the blood.

"Please act like you've been at a crime scene before," Valance said offhandedly as she crouched next to the body. "Come look at this."

Green approached to the opposite side of the powder-white corpse and squatted next to it, his eyes traveling immediately to the puncture wounds in the neck. "Anything ring a bell?" Valance asked.

"Well, there's that purple shit."

Brooks blew out a heavy breath, placing her hands on her hips. "I really thought you were full of shit, Heather."

Bannockburn, who stood in the doorway of the trailer, surveilling the surrounding structures, said, "She's still full of shit, Aliyah. Just not about this."

Brooks nodded at Green. "You've seen this before, too, haven't you?"

"Unfortunately."

She tilted her head sideways as she stared down at the body again. "That 10-87 the other day. That wasn't bullshit after all?"

Valance stood, straightening out her pants. "Oh no, that turned out to be a false alarm, but have you ever seen a clearer vampire slaying than this?" She pointed at the dead body and Brooks frowned and shook her head slowly.

Corporal turned back from the door to face the officers. "Brooks, I'm putting you in charge of interviewing the neighbors to see if anyone heard anything."

"Yes, sir." She took a step toward the doorway, and he held up a hand.

"Wait. I need to be sure we're on the same page here. You're questioning them as if you suspect a shifter, all right?"

She cocked her head to the side, squinting. "I don't think I understand. Only an idiot would think a shifter did this."

"That's not entirely true," said Bannockburn. "A person whose job depended on this not being a vampire attack might be inclined to believe a shifter did this." He paused, exchanging a concerned look with Valance. "We're not ready to call this what it is. We don't have enough yet."

"Hold on," Green said, standing up and taking two steps away from the corpse. "I have to do this bullshit *again?* I have to say a shifter did this? Vampire killings don't get much more obvious than this, sir, and you—"

"Cool it, Rookie," Valance said, setting a hand on his shoulder. "Corporal's right. The death of a human mucker isn't the hill we want to die on. It'll get brushed right under the rug, and we'll be up shit creek for trying to cause a stir."

"This is some fucked up shit," Brooks said, staring at the floor and shaking her head slowly. She looked up at the others, first at Green, then Bannockburn, and finally Valance. "I'm up to my tits in this now, aren't I?"

Valance's voice remained measured. "Are you?"

Brooks tilted her head back, staring vaguely at the ceiling and laughed morosely. "If you're asking whether I'm convinced, then yeah, I am. And I guess I got no choice but to do something about it."

Valanced stepped forward. "Good." She unbuttoned the top button of her uniform, creating enough room for her to stick her hand down and pull out a chain with leprechaun gold dangling from it. "Here. If you're going in on this, you'll need a little help."

Brooks grabbed it and held it in a flat palm as she inspected it. But unlike Green, she didn't require a helpful hint. "Goddamn. You telling me the leprechauns are part of this, too?" She glanced up at Valance. "Bless their little hearts. This is some messy shit."

"The messiest of shit," Bannockburn said, stepping forward. Brooks slid the chain over her neck and tucked it down her shirt while Bannockburn gave orders. "Brooks, I think it's best if you take this report. It was a snake shifter or something that did this. Play dumb. Everyone knows you're smarter than that, but Sergeant Montoya and Lieutenant Fukumoto will appreciate your willingness to deny flat-out what's really going on." Brooks nodded, and Bannockburn turned to the others. "You two should probably take off. Brooks and I can handle this until homicide arrives. It's a no-win situation if either of you has to deal with another vampire killing on official documents."

As Valance and Green followed orders, heading back to their car, Valance moved close to Green and said in low tones, "Sorry."

"Huh? What?" He caught himself and reeled in his surprised at hearing that word come out of her mouth in a way that didn't seem to be sarcastic like, "Sorry you're too stupid to do your job," or "Sorry that shifter tween outsmarted you."

"The other night at your apartment. Sorry about what I said."

Green blinked rapidly as memories shot to the forefront of his mind like a scalding geyser. "Which part? Because it was all unpleasant. Literally all of it."

"Ah, I dunno. Just the part where I heavily implied you'd never get a woman with a mushy yet scrawny body like yours."

He paused at the hood of his car, turning to her. "Heavily implied? You pretty much said it straight up."

She waved that off, annoyed. "You're wrong. Anyway, here's my suggestion: Brooks."

"Brooks? Suggestion for what?"

She rolled her eyes so hard they took the rest of her head with them. "Sex, Norman."

His abs clenched in a fight or flight response at the sound of his first name coming out from her mouth. "First of all, why are we having this conversation, but secondly, what in Dracula's name would give you the impression Brooks would go for it? I'm pretty sure she would *not*. So, unless you're suggesting I start sexually assaulting her as a pastime, I'm a little lost."

"You're a fucking idiot, Green. You haven't seen the way she looks at you?"

He hesitated. "What do you mean?"

"I mean she looks at you like she's undressing you with her eyes. At show-up, on duty, when you bend over to load up into your trunk each day."

"Huh." Brooks *was* hot. She had maybe a half-decade on him, but that wasn't bad. She was lean, he'd already seen her naked during the incident at Graveyard Shift, and her body had passed his (admittedly easy) test with flying colors, even though he was doing his best not to gawk. She was smart, funny, and, if he were honest, she could probably teach him a few things in bed. If she was up for it, well, hell, so was he. "You think she's into me?"

Valance grinned but didn't respond right away. Finally, she said, "Nah, I made all that stuff up about the way she looks at you. But, I mean, she might be down, and you're desperate." She leaned close and whispered, "But mostly it would be a good cover for why you two are suddenly whispering in hushed tones and visiting each other's homes like Bannockburn and I were."

"You were going to each other's homes?"

She leaned back and snapped her fingers in front of his face. "Not the main takeaway here, Rookie!" She huffed out a sharp breath and rolled her shoulders; then her tone softened again. "Are you going to do what it takes to cover for Brooks or not?"

"Yeah, yeah. Fine. I'll ask her to pretend we're banging."

"Good. It's the right thing to do. Plus, sometimes this sort of arrangement turns into actual banging. Trust me on that." She flashed a sharp smirk then stomped off.

Why? Why did she do this to him?

She was right about one thing, though: he was desperate.

Fine, he would take the suggestion and see if Aliyah was down for the act. Then, once he felt out the situation, he would do his best to make life imitate art.

For the sake of her career, of course.

CHAPTER FIFTEEN_

Montoya had hardly dismissed them from show-up when
Valance leaned forward from her spot at the back of the
meeting room and punched Green's shoulder to get his
attention. He turned in his seat, glaring at her. "What?"

"You talk to her yet?"

"Who?"

"Brooks, idiot." She nodded at the officer, who leaned
against the wall, chatting animatedly with Lawrence while
enjoying one of the donuts Marrow had brought as
punishment for leaving her badge in a department store
dressing room.

"Not yet," said Green, "but I will."

"Damn right you will. Right now." She grabbed the back
of his chair and tilted it forward, spilling him out, forcing
him to scramble to avoid sliding onto his ass on the cold
concrete floors.

"Gah! Dammit, Valance." He rolled his shoulders back,
inhaled deeply so he didn't pass out doing this simple task

of talking to a female to whom he spoke every day and whom he'd already seen naked, and marched over.

"Brooks," he said, announcing himself. "You got a second?" He grinned at her confidently, and she smiled back, her usual attitude of up-for-whatever intact.

"Yeah, sure." She turned to Lawrence. "I'll tell you the rest at lunch." Then she followed Green over to an empty corner of the room. He stood with his back to the rest of the shift so they couldn't read his lips or, more likely, his terrified expression, and leaned one arm against the wall, grinning at her like an idiot.

"What is it, Green? I still got to finish loading up."

Hell. Where did he even start? It wasn't that he hadn't considered this conversation a hundred times in the day since Valance had proposed the set-up. It was just that nothing he'd come up with sounded any good. "So, um. Last night."

That got her attention. Her gaze, which had previously wandered listlessly over his shoulder at the rest of the shift behind him, snapped onto his face. "Yeah?"

He leaned forward slightly, and so did she. "There might be some things that we have to discuss in the future, and it was suggested to me that we create a reason for us to be talking all the time." He paused, wondering where to go from there.

But, thankfully, Brooks was quick on the uptake.

She grinned. "Ah. I follow." She leaned back, letting her eyes roam from head to toe and back again. "Yeah. I could go for that."

"Hmm?" He stood up straight, removing his arm from the wall. "You could go for that?"

She shrugged a shoulder. "Sure. You're not a bad looking

guy, it *is* convenient, and, if I'm honest, I've slummed worse."

"Wait. I was just talking about"—he leaned forward so no one would overhear, and she offered up her ear —"looking like we're, you know, hooking up, so people think that's what's going on." He leaned back again, grimacing apologetically.

"Oh. Yeah, that works, too," she said.

Did she *want* more, though? Shit! He hadn't considered it a real possibility since Valance had burst his bubble the day before, the same bubble she'd created in the first place.

Man, she's a bitch.

He tried to recover. "I mean, if you want to, um, you know—"

She waved him off. "No, no. Of course not. That's unprofessional. And this is entirely professional, right?"

Nooo! "Yeah, totally. I mean, are you sure you don't want …?"

She nodded confidently. "Psh. Yeah. I just misread your meaning and didn't want to hurt your feelings. I thought *you* wanted it."

"Haha!" *Play it cool, Norman!*

She giggled, too, placing a hand on his shoulder and then sliding it down to his chest as she looked him in the eyes. Then she leaned forward and whispered, "Like this? Is this the kind of flirting you mean?"

His starched pants felt like they'd magically shrunk a size, and he swallowed down a whimper. "Yep. Just like this."

"Okay, perfect." She pulled back, staring into his eyes, her tongue wetting her lips almost imperceptibly before she sauntered away.

He turned and watched her go, wondering if he would ever stop being a complete and utter fuck-up. And how had he never noticed her perfect ass before? Like, seriously *noticed* it and given it his full attention?

At least their plan was working if the slack-jawed look on Jeremy Lawrence's handsome face was any indication.

———

Green breathed a sigh of relief as he assigned to a fairly routine call over on the south side of Fang. Or at least it appeared routine, though, that could change in the blink of an eye.

Lawrence was already on scene, having been the one to call for backup to interview the prostitute while he arrested the john.

Green pulled into the industrial parking lot two blocks off the highway and strolled up to Lawrence and the cuffed john, who sat on the curb, staring up at the handsome officer's bored face.

"I swear," the man said, "she's a siren. I couldn't do nothing about it. She picked me and then started singing that damn song, and everything just faded from my mind except me giving it to her in the backseat of my car!"

Looking over at the prostitute in question, Green's bullshit-o-meter was all the way in the red. "You talking about Stephanie over there?" he said, "She's your siren?"

The man nodded firmly. "I swear it! Please, officers, don't arrest me for this. I have a wife and family at home. If they found out, it would ruin everything I've worked so hard for. And that's hardly fair when I didn't have a choice."

Lawrence groaned. "You're a role model of personal responsibility, Mr. Brown."

"No, no," Green said, turning to Lawrence. "The man has a point. If a siren got her eye on him and decided he would be her next trick, there wasn't anything he could do about it. He's truly the victim. And if that's the case, these handcuffs should be on her, not him." He nodded over to Stephanie where she was stretched out on the hood of Lawrence's vehicle, her head propped up on one arm as she watched the conversation serenely. "Only one problem."

Mr. Brown's relieved expression sagged. "What's that?"

"Sirens are all women."

"Yeah? And?"

"And Stephen Paul Schumacher over there is not a woman by birth."

Mr. Brown's eyes shot open wide as he leaned to the side for a clear line of sight to the beautiful Stephanie where she lounged, stroking the metal of the hood with a light brush of her fingers. She blew Mr. Brown a kiss.

"No," he whispered. "No! She can't be a ... I didn't see anything when I—"

"It's called a tuck, sir," Green said, "and in the future, you might want to get a good look at the front before you rush around to the back. Or conduct business in a place with a little more light. Or maybe just admit to yourself that you're so desperate you'll ignore the obvious fact that there's something hanging between her legs that ought not to be there. Or, I dunno, not cheat on your wife at all? Man, the possibilities are endless."

As Mr. Brown fell backward onto the dirt and began crying, Green turned to Lawrence for acknowledgment of the small victory.

But Lawrence's mouth was a flat line, and his long dimples pulsated as he clenched and unclenched his jaw, stopping only to say, "Apparently, you're pretty good with the ladies, Green. Why don't you go chat up Stephanie and get her statement?"

"Um. O-kay." As far as the frequent flyers of Fang went, Stephanie was one of Green's personal favorites, mostly because she was shameless with the truth. Yes, she was exchanging sex for money. No, she had no plans for getting out. And hell yes, she knew she had warrants. Her honesty meant he almost always let her off with a warning rather than taking her in. There was no point anyway. She'd probably make more money in prison anyway.

Green backed away from Lawrence, wondering what the hell had crawled up his ass. Though even as he posed the question to himself, he already suspected he knew the answer.

———

"Booth all right?" the hostess at Greasy Griddle asked.

Brooks turned to Green, who shrugged. It wasn't ideal—it made it easier for some disgruntled asshole to ambush when there was an officer pinned by a wall—but the place was empty this late at night, and booths were much more comfortable anyway. "Yeah, that's fine," Green said.

As she led them over to a corner booth, Green slid in one side, expecting Brooks to take the other, but instead, she made him scoot over and sat next to him.

The waitress placed four menus on the table and walked away.

"What?" Brooks asked when she looked at Green. "We're

supposed to make people believe we're screwing, right? This should do the damn trick."

"Fair enough," he said, grabbing the laminated menu off the table to inspect it. "Harmon and Lawrence still coming?"

"They said they were just a couple minutes out."

Green set down the menu and twisted toward her, throwing his arm over the seat back. "Hey, here's a question. Does Lawrence hate me for some reason? I mean, I know I sound like an insecure teenager when I ask that, but he seemed a little hostile toward me earlier tonight."

"He's never mentioned anything about it to me if he does. I've always been under the impression he likes you."

Green nodded. "Yeah, I thought so, too, but I don't know anymore. It's like he's done a one-eighty."

She patted him on the collarbone, right above his bullet-proof vest. "I'm sure it's nothing. Don't overthink it."

"You're probably right. Oh! I can't believe I almost forgot. I spoke with Valance after we wrapped up a domestic violence call tonight, and—"

Motion over her shoulder drew his attention to Harmon and Lawrence arriving. Harmon flirted innocuously with the hostess while Lawrence scanned the room for the rest of his party. His eyes narrowed to two slits when he spotted Green and Brooks.

Green leaned forward, ducking out of Lawrence's line of sight. "There he is. Nope, he clearly hates me."

"I'm sure he doesn't." But her words fell flat when she turned and saw his tight expression as he stomped over. She turned back to Green. "Oh, yeah, he seems pissed. But it could just be a bad day. Don't take it personally. Oh, and *don't* bring it up," she added quickly. "Hey, Jeremy. Scoot on in."

He did so but immediately picked up the menu, saying nothing as Harmon approached the table. "Hey … you two." His eyes landed on Green's arm slung over the back of the booth, and a small grin turned the corner of his lips before he seemed to nod, accepting the new normal, and continue. "Fantasia over there says coffee's on her tonight, so drink up." He slid into the booth, forcing Lawrence to scoot over. He did so begrudgingly, making it seem like the most strenuous activity that had been asked of him all night.

"Who the hell's Fantasia?" Lawrence groused as he adjusted into his new spot on the vinyl cushion.

Harmon whapped him on the arm. "The hostess, you numb skull. The one who's way too young and pretty to be working a night shift at this shady diner." He jabbed a thumb toward Lawrence, looking at the other two. "This guy. I guess that's what happens when you're too classically handsome for your own good. You stop noticing all the beautiful young women because you're so used to every woman throwing herself at you." He chuckled and nudged Lawrence in the ribs with an elbow.

"Not *every* woman," Lawrence said, eyes glued to the menu, which Green assumed the officer would've committed to memory years ago.

Brooks shifted in the booth. "Any good calls tonight?" she asked, changing the subject.

"Ooo! Yes, actually," Harmon said excitedly. But before he could jump into it, a server approached, his eyelids drooping so severely that Green wondered if he could see them.

Fortunately, once the waiter left, Harmon's story

involved spotting Kilhaven's Most Wanted Marcus Franchioni, the were who had stabbed his brother a couple of dozen times and fled. The same one Montoya had permitted officers to shift on-sight for.

The veteran officer's abnormally upbeat mood made a lot more sense in that context. He'd just wrapped up an intense wolf-on-wolf foot pursuit across some of the wilder areas of Fang and had topped it off with an arrest. He might even be up for commendation because of it.

"So anyway," he finished, as the exhausted waiter dropped off the check and Harmon swiped it up. "So long as they don't fire me for some bullshit protocol I bypassed that no one's invoked in fifty years, I might get officer of the month for this."

"Damn, Pat," Brooks said. "I'd give my left tit for another chance to shift on duty. The freedom of stripping down, the thrill of the chase, being able to overpower someone in such a raw, primal way."

Green cleared his throat and shifted in his seat, trying to casually adjust his pants, which were a bit uncomfortable at present. When he looked up to make sure no one was looking, he noticed Lawrence also adjusting his posture.

"Thanks for getting that," Brooks said, nodding to Harmon before sliding out of the booth and stretching. "We better get out of there. No way Fang ain't lighting itself on fire tonight."

Harmon nodded and stood as well. "It *is* a Thursday after all. Frankly, I'd be disappointed in everyone if they weren't driving their cars straight into ditches and stabbing perfect strangers."

Lawrence peeled off to hit the bathroom while Green followed Harmon out of the diner. Before they made it into the parking lot, though, Brooks grabbed his arm from behind and stopped him.

"You were going to tell me something?" she said, staring up at him.

"Oh, right." She leaned back against the wall, and Green braced an arm by her head. But before he spoke, he glanced down at her chest. "That off?" he asked.

She nodded.

"Good. Corporal has a lead on a lab, but he's not ready to swoop in yet. When it comes time, though, he'll need all of us. He just has to wait for an excuse to be there and enter. When that time comes, he'll say 'luck' over the radio. That's your cue to assign to the call."

She nodded, her eyes large. "Got it. Is it weird that I'm getting a little excited just thinking about this?" She bit her bottom lip. "Kind of reminds me of being back in Ecuador. We did this kinda shit all the time."

Green chuckled. "Seems like a better reaction than wanting to piss yourself, so, yeah, I think it's fine."

"Jesus Christ, you two."

Green whirled around. Lawrence had come to a halt right outside the front door.

"Really, Aliyah? And with Officer Poncho, no less?"

"What?" Green said innocently.

Lawrence shook his head. "I just hope you don't think you're being sneaky about whatever is happening here, because *that* would be pathetic." His top lip curled into a disgusted snarl that was still annoyingly sexy.

"Lawrence," Brooks protested, "don't pull that."

He raised his hands innocently in surrender. "Don't pull what, Brooks? I'm not the one carrying on an undoubtedly unsatisfying affair with my fellow officer."

She planted her feet and stuck her lips out, giving him lethal side-eye. "Not *now* you're not."

He started down the sidewalk toward the parking lot. "Whatever. It's none of my business anyway." But he paused at Green and placed a firm, *too* firm, hand on Green's shoulder. "Just do me a favor and don't come crying to me once she's used you and moved on, okay?"

"Jeremy," she warned.

Green looked back and forth between the two. "What are you talking about? What is he talking about?"

"Nothing," Brooks growled through gritted teeth. "Nothing at all."

Lawrence guffawed. "Never a truer word was spoken." And then he released his hold of Green and sauntered out across the parking lot.

Green watched him go then turned back to Brooks.

"It was before your time, Rookie," she said.

"Care to fill me in?"

"Nope," she said, stepping around him. "I definitely do not."

CHAPTER SIXTEEN_

One of a great many reasons Fang sector rarely had a dull moment was the inspiring blend of neighborhoods. With a few exceptions, like Crown Tree, which occupied the entire northern tip of Fang, most of the sector varied dramatically from street to street when it came to the quality of homes. Two or three rows of manicured lawns with three-thousand square-foot houses could easily devolve into hundred-year-old shitheaps that had more rats than people, or, worse, more people than rats when there was a hell of a lot of rats.

It made for constant action. Because even if the crime from the low-income housing wasn't spilling over into the wealthy neighborhoods in that instant, the wealthy neighborhoods believed it was.

Which resulted in calls like the one Green was currently *en route* to, where an older werewolf bitch claimed she'd heard something rustling around in her garbage bins. And she was sure it was a shifter.

Why was she sure it was a shifter? Probably because her house backed up to the same swampland that bordered the infamous Shady Grove trailer park a mile and a half away. Call text indicated that while the woman hadn't seen the suspect, she knew it couldn't possibly be an animal from the swamp who'd been raiding her trash. No, no, it was a shifter. She was sure of it.

Bigot.

Granted, the shifters in Shady Grove were responsible for a sizable portion of the crime in Fang, but still, the elitism of some people could be a little hard to swallow.

Green hadn't wanted to assign to this call. But he'd lost himself in a sloppy fast-food hoagie in his car, and when a more exciting call came out, one from Shady Grove that reported a blood-curdling scream echoing from somewhere in the swamp, Green's hands were too greasy to touch the HAM, and by the time he'd dug the napkins out of the bag and wiped off, the call had already been snatched up by Bannockburn and Valance. So, he finished his sandwich and promised himself he'd assign to the first one that came up.

And that was this one. His plan? Show up, kiss ass, pretend to look around, then assure the woman he'd cleared a sizable radius of the land around her home, and she was officially safe.

"Mrs. Juventus?" he said when she answered the door. She scented the air and tilted her head back slightly, staring down the length of her slender nose at him.

Prejudiced taint.

"Officer Green with the Kilhaven Police. I understand you're concerned someone might be going through your trash?"

She inhaled stiffly but resigned herself the dreadful social progress that allowed a human to be a police officer.

"Yes. Around the side." She shut the door, and that was just as well; he hadn't enjoyed the brief conversation.

He clicked on his flashlight and climbed down the half-dozen steps away from her front door, rounding the corner to where she kept the garbage cans. Sure enough, one of the lids was flipped open, but that didn't necessarily mean anything.

The bloodless carcass of a river rat, though, now *that* captured Green's attention. Nutria grew large in this part of the country, and this one was bigger than most raccoons. Its body hung halfway out of the bin, eyes open wide in shock. Green parted the animal's brown fur around the neck, and with very little work, located two deep puncture wounds.

While there were some big-ass snakes in the swamp, none sucked the blood out, and none left purple goo around the bite marks. Yet, as sure as the homeless at Quick Z gas station would sexually assault another female customer, there the purple was. There was no getting around it, no pretending he didn't see it.

He'd never heard of vamps preying on non-humans, but then again, this whole situation—no, he'd call it what it was—this whole *conspiracy* was batshit insane. He might as well add vamps sucking on river rats to the growing list of weird shit he didn't know could happen.

Assuming the other call out at Shady Grove was a bust, which they often were, and not because there wasn't something substantial that had warranted the call but because of just how unhelpful everyone in that place was when the police came knocking on doors, Valance and Bannockburn, who'd assigned to it, would be just around the corner and likely unoccupied.

He grabbed his radio from his belt. "Fang 9-07. Arrived

at the report of shifter snooping. Searched around the scene, but no luck. Looks like maybe a raccoon got in."

He waited, but there was no response. Seriously? Not even Brooks? Maybe she was wrapped up in something or at a call off the highway and couldn't hear her radio over the traffic. Or maybe his code word had gone unnoticed. "9-07. No luck on this call."

Still nothing. Dammit. "Fang 9-07 to 9-01. You have any luck on that call out in Shady Grove? I'm right around the corner. I can stop by."

When Valance didn't respond at all, Green checked his radio. Yep, it was on, and it seemed to have a charge. "I repeat. No luck on my end."

More silence, then finally a voice rattled through, though not one of the ones he'd been hoping for. "Fang 9-13 to 9-07. You never struck me as someone who got lucky very often anyway."

Fucking Lawrence. His stink-eye hadn't let up in the week since the awkward lunch at Greasy Griddle. The only weight that had lifted recently was the one resulting from Green's confusion as to why Lawrence was suddenly hostile. But now Green knew. Would have been nice to know Lawrence and Brooks had a history *before* he started this charade with her. But as it was, the arrangement stuck him with all of the weirdness of hooking up with a coworker and earned him none of the sweet rewards.

He should have known Valance's ploy would only cause him grief. Everything she did caused him grief.

It was clear no one was coming to his call. Maybe the code word only worked one way? Didn't matter. He wasn't calling for backup from anyone but Valance, Bannockburn, or Brooks. Montoya wouldn't have his back on this. Despite being a werewolf, Harmon couldn't be relied upon for anything vampire related. Lawrence might actually *enjoy* watching Green drained of all his blood. With Williamson still out with his shattered knee and the hiring freeze in effect, that only left Marrow. Did he call her and bring her into the fold on the vampire stuff? She didn't seem inclined to side with them, though she was close with Brooks. Maybe Brooks could convince her.

There was no time for that, though, and it was too risky. If he trusted the wrong person with the information and it got all of them fired …

Valance knew where he lived.

No, if he valued his life at all, he would leave the major decisions to her and Bannockburn.

Granted, following the tracks of a vampire into a swamp was, in itself, a major decision and not without its own risks, but he could go slowly, feel it out, and if he did catch sight of the vamp, he could always high-tail it out of there or stake the thing.

He hurried back to his car and grabbed the retractable stake from his tactical bag, removing his silver spray to make room for the new gear. The department was so determined to ignore the threat of vamps that it had long since stopped issuing each officer a stake of his or her own. But at the insistence of Valance, he'd purchased it the month before, though this was the first time he'd attached it to his duty belt. The leather holder was stiff, and as he struggled to loop it under his belt to snap it, his self-doubt crept in.

You can't even snap a damn stake holster to your belt! What makes you think you should be going into the woods by yourself?

You're going to get yourself killed, and then Valance is going to ride the high of I-told-you-so for the rest of her life.

The click of the snap falling into place brought an abrupt end to his negative self-talk. *Okay, one obstacle down.* He was on a roll. Time to track a vampire.

The sounds of the city faded, muffled by the dense foliage, replaced by the wet sounds of the swamp. Bugs buzzed, frogs called to each other from the trees. Light from the city and the sliver of a crescent moon was unable to penetrate the canopy, and when his eyes took too long to adjust, he pulled out his flashlight and clicked it on. With one hand gripping that and the other at the ready by his belt, he crept deeper into the woods.

He struggled to keep his eyes ahead of him when every few steps landed his boot in a sludgy mud pit, making a squelching sound. He was being too noisy. He knew that. But he continued anyway. Technically, it wasn't illegal for vampires to roam around the wilder parts of Kilhaven at night, so long as they stayed away from schools, daycares, playgrounds, and places of worship other than Draculan Churches. But it *was* highly unusual for them to do so. And hunting wild animals within city limits was a misdemeanor, no matter what kind of creature you were.

It also seemed unnecessary. Vampires had access to all the blood they needed from store-bought carcasses. Most of them even had personal assistants to do the shopping for them. Why would a vampire bother to break the law to eat a nutria of all things? Could the vamp have been on a late-night stroll, decided he or she needed a snack, and grabbed the first thing available?

That was almost certainly *not* the case. Vampires lived in

nests, and the only one in Kilhaven had its own private security and wasn't technically part of the city proper, meaning KPD had no jurisdiction there. And because of the wealth of the Fanglory community, there was almost no need for them ever to leave their compound, let alone by themselves.

And Fanglory was all the way across town, nestled between Alpha and Banshee sector.

A muffled squeal ahead and to the right caused Green to freeze in his tracks. It was an animal's. Maybe another river rat, possibly a possum. A death squeal cut short; he was certain of that much. It could've been a snake that caused it. Or a gator.

Or something else.

He pulled out his gun, clicked on the scope light, and tucked his flashlight back into his belt. He needed a hand free in case he had to go for his stake.

He approached the spot where the noise seemed to have originated, but there was nothing there. He held his breath to listen, silent as death.

Then something big moved in the bushes ahead.

Snakes, even big ones, didn't cause that kind of noise, and gators didn't bother forcing their way through bushes when they were just as happy taking the path of least resistance through the mud and shallow waters.

"Fang 9-07 to 9-01," he rasped into his shoulder-mounted radio. "Any chance you're in the swamp behind Shady Grove?" It was a fool's hope, really, but then again, he'd been a fool coming in here alone, so that was appropriate.

His question was met with no response, and it occurred to him that the best way forward was the route back. He was getting too deep into the woods without backup. This was just crazy. Whatever had killed the river rat was only going after animals anyway, as far as he'd seen. There was no reason to believe it posed a threat to Kilhaven citizens, even if it *was* a vampire.

He backed up a few steps, paused, listened for more noise, but heard none, so he turned and made for the edge of the swamp, where the safety of his cruiser called to him.

Then he heard a sound. A clear one that couldn't be mistaken for anything other than the quiet weeping of a young girl.

The hair on his arms stood on end.

This changed everything.

What was a girl doing alone out here at night? Someone should have reported her missing.

Yet, he knew: *Someone already has.*

But whether that was the Pfaffs or the Holloways, he wasn't yet certain. Could this be where the vamps were keeping the missing girls? It made sense. No one came out here if they could help it, and the trees provided a reliable sound buffer if the victims were to call for help.

He couldn't leave. And he couldn't wait for backup.

Granted, charging in would be unbelievably stupid, even for him. He recognized that.

Okay, then. He would sneak up, see if he could get a read on the situation, and then get the fuck out and return with Valance and Bannockburn, even if that required driving to wherever they were, handcuffing them, and driving them over in the back of his car.

He crept forward, his heart racing wildly the nearer he drew to the pitiful whimpering.

It sounded like one voice, not two, which he prayed

didn't mean that one of the girls was already dead. Had the vamps already drained her dry then discarded her?

Caitlin Holloway's face appeared in his mind's eye, morphing almost immediately into Kim's face. The two looked so similar his brain couldn't keep them straight.

But as he arrived at the edge of a narrow clearing, and saw a small girl hunched over in a strip of mud, covered in smudges of it up to her waist, he identified her, without a single doubt, as Caitlin. Her profile matched the girl in the photos, the ones that remained in the center console of his personal vehicle because he couldn't bear to throw them out but couldn't yet bring himself to face the Holloways long enough to hand them back.

Caitlin wasn't bound or restrained in any way he could see from his angle behind her. Had they set her free? God, what had happened to her?

She continued to sob as she crouched in the mud. He looked around for any other being present but found none.

Perhaps she was lost. Maybe she was hiding from whatever had raided Mrs. Juventus's trash can.

Or maybe it was a trap. Could she be bait? It *was* almost too easy. If he rushed forward to comfort her, would vampires descend on him from all sides? He should turn around and get Valance. Caitlin had survived this long. Maybe she could last another half hour.

He'd just made up his mind on the matter when the little girl turned, and her eyes found him. "Who are you?" she asked.

Blood dripped down her face and shirt, but it was immediately clear to Green that she was in no physical danger. That wasn't her blood. He, on the other hand, was mightily screwed.

Her eyes shone red. They weren't bloodshot. They were red.

Green had made a crucial error. Well, a bunch of crucial errors, all of which had led him to stand at the edge of a clearing in a soundproof swamp with a tiny blood-covered vampire child.

Like baby copperheads, he remembered Bannockburn explaining. Deadly. Indiscriminate.

But she seemed quite the opposite at the moment, more docile than bloodthirsty.

Although, Green would be the first to admit he knew very little about child psychology. In general, he was terrible with kids. Something about their honesty threw him off-step.

And he knew even less about child vamp psychology. How much humanity was there left in Caitlin Holloway? Could he appeal to it? If he asked her to come with him, would she? Was there a way to rehabilitate her? Maybe even change her back? Heal her?

"I'm Norman," he said. "I've been looking for you. Your parents are worried about you."

She straightened from her crouch and stared at the ground by her feet, hugging herself. "I miss them."

"You can come with me, and I'll take you to them." He took a careful step closer.

She took a step back. "They won't want to see me. Not anymore."

"Are you kidding? You're their daughter. They'll love you no matter what."

She looked up at him, her crimson eyes harboring both a chilling intensity and a frightening vacancy. "I've been killing. They won't like that."

"I've killed someone before," he said. "Sometimes you have to. But the people who love you will understand. They understood when I did it." He decided not to mention the fact that, actually, no, his parents did *not* understand and hadn't spoken to him since the incident. He also decided not to mention how big of a relief it was to be rid of his family ties.

Except for Kim.

He stepped closer to Caitlin and this time she didn't move away. What resemblance she'd shared with Kim was now eclipsed by those eyes. They changed the entire look of her face. Maybe she was no longer Caitlin at all.

"They won't understand," she said. "And I'll kill them too."

"Uh, what?" He stopped in his tracks. "No, no, you wouldn't kill them."

"Yes, I would." She grinned. "I think about it all the time now." Her arms fell against her body, and she tilted her head to the side. "You're a human."

He let go of the gun with his left hand, which he lowered toward his belt.

She grinned, her fangs peeking out beneath her top lip. "I could kill you, too."

"Do you want to?" he asked, taking another step back. Keeping her engaged while he increased the distance between them might be his only way out of this mess.

"Yes," she said plainly. "I do."

"You don't have to. It looks like there are plenty of other animals around here you could drink."

She spat, sending a spray of diluted blood his direction. "They taste like moldy fruit. No, humans are much better."

She grinned, and Green guessed this conversation was reaching its end.

He held out his left hand, signaling for her to stop. "I can help you find humans. Ones that taste better than me." It was a desperate attempt to buy himself some time. Luckily, his body mic wasn't recording, because *if* he made it out alive, that wasn't something he'd want going in public records. And if he *didn't* make it out alive, those weren't the best last words.

"I don't know. You smell pretty delicious to—"

The wooden stake shot out of her stomach, snagging her intestines and pulling them out, skewered on the end.

"What the fuck!" Green shouted, snatching his own stake from his belt, flicking his wrist to extend it, and holding it out in front. "What the fucking fuck!"

A sound like screeching tires rose up from Caitlin Holloway, and she crumpled to the ground.

"Shut your goddamn mouth, Rookie," said a voice on the other side of the clearing. Valance emerged next to Bannockburn, who held a long, hollow metal tube in front of him. Coming from the end was a thin metal cable attached to the end of the stake that jutted out from Caitlin's face-down body.

"*What the shit is that?*" He demanded, holding both his gun and stake in front of him.

"Holster your weapon, Green," Bannockburn said, hustling forward to the body. Valance and the corporal converged on the baby vamp, the former driving her stake into Caitlin's back for good measure. "Yeah, she's dead."

Green switched his gun out for a flashlight. "Is that a goddamn vampire harpoon?" he asked, still gaping at the thing Bannockburn held in his hands.

"Stop. Yelling," Valance insisted.

Bannockburn shrugged. "Yeah, I guess it is. Never thought of it like that."

With that question answered, Green returned his attention to the tragedy at hand. "You killed her."

"You're welcome," Valance said. "She was about to kill you, dumbass. Also, what was that shit about better tasting humans? That's pretty fucked up."

Bannockburn yanked his stake free and reloaded it into the cylinder. "Agreed," he said. "But we have more pressing matters. We need to get rid of this body."

Valance braced a boot on Caitlin's back for leverage as she pulled her stake free.

"No, no, no," Green said. "That's not really what we're going to do. Right?" He scanned Bannockburn's expression for reassurance but found none.

Valance was no help either, staring at him like she normally did, as if he had a serious brain defect she was only just discovering. "No one would blame you for killing a vampire that was about to kill me. I'll say she was charging." She wiped the blood off her stake using the large fronds of a nearby fern. "I take that back. Everyone's going to blame us for killing a vampire child. Literally everyone."

"It's true," Bannockburn added. "I don't feel good about what I just did. In fact, it'll probably haunt my dreams for years, if not the rest of my life. But that poor girl was already dead, far as I'm concerned. Our job is to keep the people of Kilhaven safe, and with her on the loose, no one was.

"She also happens to be compelling evidence that vampires are stealing human children, and trust me when I say we're still not ready for that shoe to drop in the newspapers. The panic that would ensue would be the opposite of public safety."

"So the Holloways will never know what happened to their daughter?"

Bannockburn scratched his chin with his thumb, leaving a small smudge of blood behind. "They'll learn eventually. But not yet." He crouched beside Caitlin's body, sighing heavily. "I don't like this, Rookie, and I don't expect you to like it either, but I need you to understand it." He looked up at Green. "Do you understand it?"

"God dammit," Green groaned, looking down at the slain vamp. "God … Yes, I understand it." He pressed the release button and compressed the stake, smashing it at each end before jamming it back into its holster. "Let's get this over with."

Bannockburn glanced at Valance, who nodded her solemn approval. "Okay, yeah," he said. "Glove up. We need to move her farther into the swamp. The gators should take care of the rest before anyone ventures back here and finds her."

Valance was the first with gloves on, and she rolled the girl onto her back and stared down at her face. "We better put together something soon, Bruce. I can't keep doing this. This shit is even making *me* wanna vomit, and I spent three years down in—"

"South America," Bannockburn finished for her. "Yeah, we know."

CHAPTER SEVENTEEN_

Green dreamed of a day when an attractive woman showed up on his doorstep and it had nothing to do with vampires.

Today wasn't that day.

Brooks stood on the old welcome mat that had been there since before he moved into the apartment and might have chemically bonded with the concrete floors by now. Seeing her in jeans and a lavender tank top was as jarring as seeing Valance in her street clothes, and for a second, he forgot why he'd invited her over.

Oh right. That small murdered child we dumped in the swamp last night.

"Come on in," he said.

The fact that he'd been unable to sleep worked to the advantage of his apartment, as he'd spent the last few hours straightening and scrubbing the place from top to bottom.

If only Valance could see it now.

Then, *Who cares what Valance thinks about my apartment?*

Brooks made her way into the living room right off the

front door and was already standing by the couch when Green gestured for her to have a seat.

"Everything okay?" Brooks asked as she took a seat on his lopsided couch, making the wise decision of sitting on the end closest to the ground.

He paced in front of the coffee table. "Obviously not, or else I wouldn't have invited you here."

"Christ, Green, what's crawled up your ass?"

"Huh?" He looked up at her, realized what he'd just said and apologized. "Sorry, sorry. It was a weird night."

"I figured. Lawrence mentioned that you were babbling on about luck, and then I realized you were probably calling for me, but by the time I was able to get off the family violence call, you were already back at the substation. Another false alarm?" She leaned forward. "Oh shit, did Valance sucker you in again?"

"No. She didn't. And it wasn't a false alarm." He rounded the table and sat on the couch next to her, bracing himself so the incline didn't roll him too close.

"Holy hell," she said. "What happened?"

"I need to know you're serious about working with us on this thing."

"I am," she said, the lines around her eyes softening with concern. "Is everyone okay?"

"We found Caitlin Holloway," he blurted.

But Brooks shook her head vaguely. "Who?"

"One of the missing girls from Crown Tree."

"I ain't heard nothing about that. Seems like—"

"She's dead."

Brooks gasped, and he couldn't help but admire that small act. Someone he worked with was still affected by the death of a child. Good to know. Maybe becoming callous wasn't an inevitable eventuality after all.

He rushed into the story from the point where he arrived at Mrs. Juventus's home to when they burned their uniforms in a dumpster, switching into their backup uniforms—not the intended use of said backups, he was sure. Brooks chewed her top lip but listened silently until he finished.

"Valance didn't tell me I could tell you, so if she asks, you don't know," he finished.

She set her palm on his cheek, looking into his eyes. "You can do things without Valance's permission, you know." She let her hand fall to her lap and leaned back against the armrest of the couch. "We're in the shit now." She stared thoughtfully toward the back hallway of his apartment.

"Yeah," he said, chuckling gravely. "We are."

She pressed her lips together, sucking in air through her nose. Her chest rose, and he struggled to keep his eyes off it. Now was not the time.

"Well," she said, "we've been through shit together before, huh? We did both shoot a human not that long ago."

Their eyes met, and they laughed. It felt dangerous, yet Green's shoulders relaxed for the first time in hours.

"And I was technically shot in the process," she added, causing them both to laugh harder.

Green pulled it together, saying, "We're probably gonna die, aren't we?"

With one last giggle, Brooks wiped a tear from her eye. "Yeah, probably." She gazed into his eyes again. "But everyone's gotta die sometime."

Something was happening. He could feel it but couldn't find the words as he stared into Aliyah's eyes. "Yeah, I guess so."

"Sometimes awful things seem inevitable, yet there's that little hope you can't get rid of that says you can escape, that it's not inevitable if you play your cards just right. At least with death, you know it's inevitable, so there's no use worrying about it." When she placed a hand on his knee, it clicked into place *exactly* what was happening.

He tried to imagine what came next: she would be the one to lean forward first because he lacked the gonads, but he would meet her in the middle. Their lips would crash into each other's, and it wouldn't take long for it to escalate. Would they move to the bedroom, or maybe they'd shed their clothes here and move to the bedroom for the next round?

She leaned forward, and rather than meeting her, he said, "I can't," and felt acid roil in his stomach as soon as the words left his lips. "It's not that I don't want to," he said hurriedly, "it's just that— I don't know. There's so much going on; I don't trust myself not to fuck up every decision I make right now."

Her eyes darted down to his lips then back again, and she nodded. "I get it. That's fine." She leaned back. "That's better." She frowned sympathetically and patted his knee. "Valance and Bannockburn are probably off somewhere fucking each other into a coma."

"Wait. I thought it was just a cover. You really think they're—"

"*Oh* yeah. No doubt. But they're a different breed."

"Timberwolf?"

"Well, yes, that. What I mean is that they're a different breed of *person*. They can shut it off, you know? It's useful, but it's scary as hell, a dark kind of life. You're not like that. Maybe it makes this job harder for you, but I, for one, am glad to see it in someone. And I don't think it's just because you're a rookie, either, Norman. I think it's who you are."

"Human?" he asked.

"No. Just … I don't know. Caring. Thoughtful."

God, he was an idiot. Why had he stopped her? All he wanted at that moment was to be like Valance or Bannockburn so he could shut off the trauma and indulge in Aliyah. "And you're like me? We're the same breed?"

She placed a hand on his chest, over his heart, staring down at it thoughtfully. Then she shook her head. "No, Norman. I'm like them no matter how much I wish I weren't." When she stood and headed toward the door, he called out to her.

"Hold on."

She paused and looked back at him, arching an eyebrow but letting him continue.

"Can I have a do-over? I can turn it off for, like, ten minutes. A half-hour?"

She chuckled. "Not long enough."

"If I were a different breed, though, would this be one of those inevitable things?" He waved his hand between the two of them.

"Oh yeah," she said. "It would be going down as we speak. Then it'd go down a few more times."

Fuck. "So, um. What if I'm a different breed tomorrow?"

She rolled her eyes. "Sure, Green. If you magically learn to compartmentalize *and* we have another moment like the one we just had, then it'll happen."

He narrowed his eyes at her, trying to understand. "A moment, like … What do you mean exactly?" He had to know if he was going to spend the next twenty-four hours orchestrating it.

But she shook her head then let herself out.

CHAPTER EIGHTEEN_

"Fang 9-80. 9-01 and I had no luck locating the suspect at the given address, but another resident provided an address over on Musgrave, behind Feeney's. We're going to head that way, see if we can catch up with him."

Fuck. This is getting old.

But Bannockburn had invoked the code word. So now, despite a long night functioning off of zero sleep, thanks to a nightmarish montage of images from the slain vampire girl mingled with what might have been with Brooks repeating through his mind for the past sixteen or so hours, he had to drive clear across sector to the edge of Ecto and to locate Bannockburn's vehicle parked somewhere on Musgrave.

Would Brooks be heading that way, too? His stomach knotted at the thought of it. He'd only seen her briefly in show-up earlier that night, and she'd smiled and joked around with him and the others like nothing had happened.

Which was, of course, true and exactly what she should've done. But still.

The two cop cars weren't exactly difficult to find. They

were parked halfway on the sidewalk of a row of industrial warehouses with fenced in lots.

Bannockburn and Valance huddled by her car, speaking in low tones as Green approached. "What's going on?"

They turned their attention to him, and Bannockburn jumped right into it. "We got a lead on a shipment."

"Hold up," Valance interrupted nodding at something behind Green. "Brooks is here."

The other car park next to his. Once Brooks had joined them, Bannockburn jumped back into it.

"Shipment of the drug is going out. They call it sprinkles. All we're doing tonight is watching, though. No action. You got that?" He looked directly at Valance as he said it.

She held up her hands innocently. "Don't have to tell me twice. Those Irish fuckers don't play around with their fighting sticks. Never has there been a clearer example of overcompensation if you ask me."

"Our objective is to figure out how this operation runs. Once we know that, we'll have a lot of options open up for how we want to play this. If there's an opportunity to sneak in, grab some samples or other crucial intel, we can do that, but *only* if there's an easy opening. It's imperative that we go completely undetected, got it?"

Green nodded and looked at Brooks, who nodded as well.

Bannockburn held up a hand. "That being said, if shit hits the fan, you need to be ready to fight. We know the leprechauns are predominantly in charge of this, but there could also be vamps. If that's the case, you run like the fucking wind. Vamp killing here will not be as easy as, um —" His eyes darted to Brooks.

"She knows," Green said sheepishly. "I told her. This morning."

"There's a story I'd like to hear," Valance mumbled.

If Corporal minded that Green had taken it upon himself to fill in Brooks, he didn't show it. "So you know, and you still came. That tells me all I need to know." He nodded respectfully at Brooks. "Okay. Ready?"

Bannockburn led the way down the block to one of the larger lots. The chain-link was already cut, and he pulled it back and let them through first.

They approached the warehouse, guns drawn, with Bannockburn and Valance front and center, Green and Brooks on the flanks, until they reached a set of heavy metal doors. Ten feet above ground level was a small window, and light shone out from it into the dark night, but there was no way they could see inside. Bannockburn wedged his fingers between the two doors and slowly slid one back. There was a slight grinding of metal on metal as it moved on its track; but the sound blended with the noise coming from inside.

They slipped into the warehouse.

Just beyond the door were three large drums, tall and wide enough for the four officers to hide behind. One at a time, they darted over, keeping toward the black metal walls, where their navy blue uniform blended in. Bannockburn was the last over, and the four of them paused until they were sure no one had seen them. There was little chance anyone had at this angle and distance from the main floor, but the importance of it made this a classic case of better safe than sorry.

Bannockburn peeked around one of the drums, scoping out the cavernous room. He motioned for each of them to also take a look and familiarize themselves with the lay of the land.

When it was Green's turn, he inhaled deeply and then peeked out just enough to get both eyes on the scene.

Most of the warehouse was devoted to four long tables running the width of it, at each of which a half dozen leprechauns worked, their backs to him as they faced heaping piles of purple powder. They cut, measured, bagged, and sealed, then tossed the large packages into what looked like industrial-sized laundry baskets. When one of the baskets filled up past the brim, the leprechaun nearest stopped what he was doing, grabbed it, and wheeled it away into a back room.

"According to the cherubim, they double-check and stamp each one," Bannockburn whispered. "Sprinkles is said to be like snorting cocaine mid orgasm. Sounds great, assuming you don't have a bad reaction and explode. It's obliterating the cherubim cocaine sales. Obviously, they're not happy about that. Hence ratting to the police."

Just off the main room was a series of doors, one of which was open. The space was set up as an office, one fit for an accountant or some such boring job.

Green huddled closely with the other three officers as Bannockburn explained the plan. "Our man in the cherubim said the shipment is scheduled for three twenty a.m. The driver and his men will be coming inside to inspect the operation, after which they'll head outside to load up. Once the show is over, the workers will either head home or take a break. If we have an opportunity to nab some evidence, that'll be it."

Green looked at his watch. It was five after three. Fifteen minutes of hiding out, then it would be show time.

Maybe.

"Everyone have their coin?" Bannockburn asked. "You're gonna need it."

Valance nodded like *duh*. Green hadn't taken his off since he'd first gotten it, not even to shower. He preferred to think of it as an act of diligence rather than one of fear.

He looked at Brooks, who grimaced and shook her head. "I think I left it in my locker back at the sub."

Bannockburn shut his eyes, and Valance was forced to bite her fist to hold in her displeasure.

Green decided to take a more proactive approach, reaching two fingers down his collar and pulling out his chain, which he slipped off over his head and held out to her. "Here. Just take mine. I already have shit luck."

But Brooks pushed it away. "Hell no. I'll be fine."

"Come on. I can't let you go in unprotected," he said, moving it toward her again.

"Hey," she said sharply, "don't be sexist. I'm more experienced than you and a hell of a lot more dangerous. Drop the chivalry."

Valance snorted quietly, and Green shot her a dirty look.

The matter was settled, or so everyone but Green seemed to assume.

But when Valance stepped forward to get another peep at the operation, leaving Green at the rear, he crouched low, and delicately slid up Brooks's pant leg, so that he could slip the coin into the back of her boot. He knew she would feel it the moment he let go, so he intentionally nudged her calf at the same moment.

She turned and glared down at him. "What are you doing?" she hissed.

"Sorry. A bit cramped back here. My boot was untied." He stood up, and she let the matter drop.

Bannockburn and Valance took shifts watching the process on the main floor, while Green kept an eye on the space behind them. There wasn't much, just a few feet and then the metal wall. An emergency exit door was back and to the left, and that seemed like a good thing to keep in mind, in the unfortunate event that things went very south very quickly, which was usually the rate at which everything fell to hell.

Valance stepped away, and Brooks took her place to get another look, as she did so, Valance ran a few careful fingertips over her slicked-back hair as she stared thoughtfully at the cement floor.

The sound of a large truck outside pulled Green's attention back to the task at hand, and he tiptoed over to stand close behind the corporal.

Someone hit him on the arm, silently but firmly, and he turned around to see Valance staring at him like he had some explaining to do. He mouthed, "What?" and she pointed down at Brooks's boot.

The chain Valance had given him at his apartment hung out the bottom of her pants leg. *Crap.*

"Fucking idiot," Valance mouthed. The phrase was so familiar coming from her that he had no problem reading her lips. She reached down the back of her uniform and grabbed her own chain, pulling it over her head and holding it out to him. "Take it," she whispered.

He shook his head. "Keep it. I'm fine."

"There's no evidence to support that," she hissed. The coin remained gripped in her fist, the chain dangling from the bottom. She shook it at him. "Take the damn thing!" she whispered.

He gritted his teeth. She wouldn't let this go, would she? Fine then.

He reached for it, but it never made it into his grasp.

A shillelagh cracked into Valance's side, the blow landing just beneath her extended arm in a sickening crunch.

Green whirled around just in time to duck the second blow as the leprechaun swung the fighting stick again. It struck the metal drum instead, and Bannockburn bum-rushed the little guy to neutralize the attack. But it was already too late. They'd been outed.

That was the start of everything going to shit. And quick.

Once Bannockburn had his arms around the leprechaun, holding him in place even as he sustained blunt jabs in the ribs from the wooden stick, Brooks fired her Taser into the Irishman's side, causing him to crumple and drop his weapon. Bannockburn kicked it away, sending it clattering, and Brooks slapped on the cuffs and stood again in a flash.

On the other side of the drums, frenzied footsteps slapped the floors like raindrops on a tin roof, and shouts in a language Green didn't recognize echoed through the room, assaulting him from every angle at once.

He turned toward the emergency exit. They could get out that way. More likely, though, that was where this shitty little guy had come from, and there would be more waiting on the other side.

"We need to scare them off before they arm themselves properly," said Bannockburn. He turned to Brooks. "Ready?"

"Yep. Let's go get the snot knocked out of us, Corporal."

He grabbed his radio. "Fang 9-80. Stumbled upon some

serious trouble at 540 Hargrove. 10-45 in progress. Requesting backup."

When Brooks spoke into her radio, Green couldn't help but admire her calm tone. "Fang 9-02 to 9-80. I'm in the area. Heading your way."

Valance, who grimaced, sucking in air as she straightened up off the floor, got her feet under her, clutching her ribs where the shillelagh had landed with one hand while operating her radio with the other. "Fang 9-01. On my way, 9-80."

"You okay?" Green asked her, once Bannockburn and Brooks had sprinted away, shouting. "Kilhaven Police! Stop where you are!"

She nodded but then cringed and groaned as she stepped forward.

"Fang 9-07," Green called in. "Just finished up a report. Heading that way."

Ecto officers were soon chiming in as well, and Green knew they didn't have much time now.

Despite the rush, Valance made the time to reach down, pull her Taser from her belt and fire it into the cuffed suspect, causing him to thrash for the few seconds of charge.

While Green didn't support using force like that on a restrained suspect, he also knew the leprechaun was lucky he got off with a simple tasing after assaulting Valance like he had.

As the leprechaun moaned, she seemed satisfied. "Okay, let's go. Hit those side offices first."

With no clue who or what might be behind the closed doors, the obvious first choice was the open one, and Green led the way, clearing the room as quickly as he could with Valance providing cover.

With all the scrambling to dispose of evidence, and with the stir Bannockburn and Brooks were causing, veritable giants that they seemed in present company, Green and Valance were able to cut through the room without interference.

"Clear," he said, and she moved in behind him, yanking open every drawer she could as he kept his gun leveled at the door.

As the ruckus in the main room subsided, the sound of dozens of tiny footsteps was replaced by a strange, repetitive but arrhythmic thumping. Then a few more thuds like a sack of flour falling from a tall shelf, then silence. That was either a good sign or a bad sign; both seemed equally as likely.

Green didn't have to wait long before Valance said they were good to go and he stepped out to see what was going on.

Brooks and Bannockburn had wrangled and tied up two leprechauns each using the disposable zip ties they carried for situations just like this, where there might not be enough handcuffs to go around. "The truck got away," Brooks said, winded, pinning both of her suspects on the ground with her knees. When one of them squirmed against her, she inhaled sharply, her face screwing up in pain.

"You okay?" Green asked.

"Yeah, just took a hit with one of those damn sticks. I'll be fine, though."

But once the sirens approached, red and blue lighting the ceiling of the warehouse through the high windows, and Brooks tried to stand, her leg gave out beneath her.

"Aw shit." She stumbled and reached out to catch herself before she went face first into the hard floor.

One of her suspects took the opportunity to scramble to his feet and take off at a sprint, his hands still bound behind his back. Green couldn't help but admire the foolish hope inherent in such an act.

Unfortunately for the leprechaun, Valance was a quick draw with the Taser, and he only made it a few steps before she nailed him, the two prongs landing perfectly, one sinking into the skin on his lower back, the other into his right hamstring. He seized up and fell facefirst immediately. "I got these two," Valance said. "Green, will you help Brooks out of here?"

He threw her arm over his shoulder and acted as a crutch as they left the warehouse and met the new arrivals in the parking lot.

"You did good in there, Rookie," she said, gritting her teeth.

"Same to you." And he couldn't help but feel a new level of warmth and fondness for Brooks, who'd gotten herself injured, yet again, on a call with him, but didn't show an ounce of resentment toward him because of it.

"Now get your story rock solid," she added, "and don't fuck us all, please."

He almost dropped her as he reflexively jerked back to get a better look at her. "Why do you assume I'm going to do that?"

"Because you're the only one out of the four of us who lacks substantial on-the-job lying experience. Sure, you've done it once or twice, but you ain't got nothing on the rest of us."

"Stop," Green said. "You're a clean cop."

"Well, sure. But in the military? If you think anyone coming out of South America isn't a practiced liar, you need to read up on your military history. We were asked to do some pretty dumb shit."

Fair enough. "Well, I won't fuck everyone. So don't worry about that."

"Officer Brooks," said Corporal Singh, approaching. "You injured?"

"Yes, sir, but I'm sure it's fine. Just a bruise. Took a shillelagh to the shin."

He winced but nodded and ushered them over to where one of the Ecto officers had spread out an emergency blanket for any casualties. "Rest here." As he left them, crossing the abandoned parking lot toward the empty warehouse, he rattled off orders over his radio to the other Ecto officers on scene.

"Let's take a look at it," Green said, clicking on his flashlight. The first thing he noticed was the pitch-black spot standing out against the faded navy of her pants.

"Is that blood?" he asked.

"Nah," she said as Green gently rolled up her uniform. "Probably just—whoops. Yep, guess it is."

Green turned his eyes skyward as quickly as he could, but not before the image of Brooks's protruding tibia was seared into his brain forever.

"Huh," she said. "Guess I *am* injured."

"Jesus hell," Valance shouted from a few feet away, where she held a cuffed leprechaun by the wrists in each hand. "They got you good. Corporal, you see that?" she hollered over her shoulder to Bannockburn.

He caught up and turned his gaze toward it. "My God, Brooks. I'm not a doctor, but that shit looks broken."

"I'd say it looks more like six weeks of paid leave," Valance said.

One of the leprechauns chuckled in his tinny, high-pitched voice, and Valance shook him by the cuffs until he stopped and began rambling in a language Green didn't understand.

"Hey," Valance said. "Knock it off!"

But the leprechaun didn't stop.

"I said *knock it off.*" She landed an elbow between his shoulder blades.

"Valance," Green said.

"I will tase you again, sir," she shouted at the top of the little man's head. But that didn't stop him either, so she pulled her Taser from her belt, the cartridge having been discarded after the last use, and pressed it against him, prepping for a dry fire that would do the trick.

The leprechaun stopped chattering. "Easy, bitch. I was just singing an old folk tune."

"Like hell you were." She stared at Bannockburn, the faintest hint of fear in her eyes. "I'm taking this recording back to the station, and we'll see what the interpreters have to say about your folk tune. My guess is you're about to tack on an additional count of assaulting a police officer to your list of felony charges." She shoved him forward. "I'll tase you again the second you open your mouth. Be warned." She gritted her teeth. "Shit. I *knew* this would happen. God dammit."

Green watched her leave with the two suspects, his mouth hanging open slightly. He turned to Bannockburn. "Did she just— Did we just— Was that a curse?"

The corporal sighed heavily. "*Oh* yeah. We'll just have to wait and see what kind once they translate it. Thankfully the only person who has to worry about it is the one who forgot to wear her coin." He frowned at Brooks. "Sorry, Aliyah. Maybe it was nothing major. Like you can't have children until it's lifted or something."

"If only I could be so fortunate," she said, staring down at her broken leg. "KPD's insurance for women's health ain't exactly ideal. That kinda curse could save me a lot on copay."

"We'll figure it out," Bannockburn assured her. "Just lie low, not that you'll have much of a choice, until we can get a court order to make him reverse it." Corporal led his suspects over to his cruiser.

Bannockburn didn't know. He still thought Green had been wearing their protection and Brooks was the vulnerable party. He was almost too afraid to move until he could figure out what kind of a curse had been set upon him.

Valance returned with a paramedic, who knelt down and began stabilizing Brook's injury for transport.

"First getting shot and now this," Valance said. "It's almost like your leg is cursed."

Brooks laughed through her pained expression. "Maybe your suspect was just *reversing* a curse."

"Doubt that." Valance crossed her arms over her bulky vest. "But also, it wouldn't have worked." She nodded down at Brooks's boot, and Brooks had to look past her bloody shin to see what Valance was talking about. She grabbed the chain and pulled it out until the gold medallion fell and dangled in the air. Looking from Valance to Green, her nostrils flaring slightly as deep lines formed at the corners of her eyes, she said, "Which one of you dumb-asses did that?"

Valance jabbed a finger at Green who cringed. "Sorry. I just didn't—"

"Idiot," Brooks said, shaking her head. "You think I ain't never been cursed before? I know how to handle a damn curse. I pissed off more *brujos* in the war than you can count on all your fingers and toes."

"I tried to give him mine," Valance said, "but that ginger prick smacked me with his cock compensation stick before this knight in shining armor could grab it. Damn thing flew out of my grasp, ended up who knows where."

Green stood quickly. "Wait, does that mean you didn't have it on just now?"

"No, Detective." She shook her head to clear it. "Oh wait, that's my bad. You're so good at stringing together disparate pieces of information; I got you confused with Detective Obvious." He nodded back toward the warehouse. "It's still somewhere inside, and now I get to go find it before crime scene does and starts asking questions." She addressed the paramedic. "You didn't hear that, Lewis."

He nodded obediently.

"Does that mean you might be cursed, too?" Green asked.

"We'll soon find out, won't we?"

He'd managed to leave himself *and* Valance without protection. Great. He supposed the least he could do was try to help her clean up after his mistake. "If you distract them," he said, "I'll grab the medallion." He took a decisive step toward the warehouse, tripped over his boots, and fell forward, hardly catching himself before his chin slammed into the asphalt.

The distinct ripping coupled with the extra room in his

pants didn't leave much of a mystery as to what had happened.

He jumped up, trying to cover the rip in the crotch, and as he did so, his duty belt snapped.

He reached for it to keep it from clattering to the ground, weapons and all.

Before he could, the belt holding up his uniform pants snapped.

His pants fell to mid-thigh before he could catch up with them.

"What the— Shit. How did—"

Brooks chuckled, but Valance shook her head somberly. "So it begins," she said. "Go grab your spare and I'll meet you inside."

But as she turned, one of her knees buckled, and his composed, arguably respectable former FTO dropped like a bag of rocks, as her cry of "Son of a taint!" echoed through the parking lot.

CHAPTER NINETEEN_

Short staffed didn't even begin to describe the paltry numbers of the Fang 900s. With the hiring freeze still in effect, retirements, transfers, Williamson's and Brooks's leave, and Valance's thus far unexplained absence (though Green suspected it was due in part to not wanting to make a fool of herself in front of her shift mates while the curse was still in full swing), it was a good time to be a criminal in their busy sector.

Montoya said as much at show-up at the start of the following workweek.

"High priority calls only. Let day shift respond to any remaining low priority calls in the morning. If someone's not bleeding profusely or about to, don't assign. We can't have you getting tied up in a he-said-she-said domestic abuse call to the same address you responded to yesterday and last week and the week before. And *definitely* no stolen vehicle calls." He sighed, his eyes roaming the few faces that remained. "Also, on behalf of Chief Spinner, I'd like to announce a few commendations. These are all for bravery, quick thinking, and effective de-escalation of a potentially deadly situation at the drug lab last week." He reached behind him and pulled certificates from the table, reading off one at a time. "Officer Norman Green."

Lawrence, Harmon, Marrow, and Bannockburn clapped halfheartedly.

"Green," Montoya said more forcefully, shaking the piece of paper at him.

"Oh! That's me. Sorry." He jumped up from his chair and grabbed his official commendation.

"Corporal Bruce Bannockburn."

As the rest clapped, Bannockburn waved it off. "I'll grab it later," he said from his usual spot against the back wall.

Montoya frowned, displeased with Bannockburn's lack of enthusiasm for the fanfare, and set Bannockburn's certificate face down on the table. "And then Officer Aliyah Brooks and Officer Heather Valance, neither of which is here right now." He flipped those over onto Bannockburn's.

"Yeah, about that," Lawrence asked. "Where is she?"

"Who?" said Montoya.

"Valance. I know Brooks got injured, but I don't remember hearing anything about Valance."

The only minor miracle of the whole leprechaun clusterfuck was that news of Green and Valance's curse hadn't already made the rounds through departmental gossip channels. This had been at the request of Montoya, who'd arrived on scene not long after the Ecto officers and had immediately insisted that if Green were to remain working, accepting a hefty hazard pay, he not worry his shift mates about his "condition," as the sergeant had called it.

Montoya nodded, but avoided eye contact with Lawrence

when he mumbled, "She reported psychological trauma and is using up some of her paid leave to recuperate."

Lawrence's mouth fell open. "HA! I dunno, Sarge. Are we talking about the same nightmare of a woman? Pretty sure Valance doesn't have emotions like the rest of us."

Montoya's nostrils turned into two large caverns as his lips pursed for a split second before replying. "What do you want me to say, Jeremy? She asked for time off for the first time in a decade, and she had that look in her eyes that—" He snapped his mouth shut, swallowed, and continued with more professional composure. "She's earned a break. Your input is unnecessary. Thank you." The sergeant smacked the on button of the projector. "Okay, so, thanks to the work of the commended officers, we've officially identified *sprinkles*, the newest street drug. The results haven't come back from the lab about the chemical makeup, but that doesn't matter to us anyway. The important thing is that we now know the official cause of death of the shifter Mark Frist and the leprechaun Kevin Walsh."

"Were those the ones that exploded?" Harmon asked.

Montoya shut his eyes as if bracing himself against a fist to his round gut and clenched his jaw briefly. "Yes, Officer Harmon, those were the two victims who exploded."

"And you're sure it was sprinkles and not Green? I mean, he was cradling both of them when they died." Grinning, Harmon winked at Green like blaming him for two horrific deaths was a funny joke shared between old friends.

Green forced a smile in return.

Montoya ignored the question entirely. "With this new knowledge, there will be forthcoming updates to the procedure on how to deal with such cases, though we suspect that by shutting down the operation on Hargrove Street, we've effectively cut off the supply to Kilhaven."

"For now, though, we're stuck with the poncho thing still?" Marrow asked.

"Yes, Officer Marrow. We're sticking with the *poncho thing* until we can get an official recommendation."

"Good," she said, nodding. "I like the poncho thing. It pairs well with the persistent futility of working in this goddamn sector."

———

"Should I even ask you how your weekend went?" Bannockburn said, sneaking up behind Green as he bent down to pick up his tactical bag only to have the strap break and the contents scatter across the parking lot.

Green had managed to make it through show-up and to his squad car in the substation parking lot without any unlucky things happening, making it his longest streak of the day. He supposed he should be grateful, but it was difficult to feel that as he surveyed his gear spread out on the asphalt. He ought to pick it up right away, considering how expensive most of his equipment was to replace, but decided the best course of action, considering his condition, was not to do anything at all.

From his excruciatingly long shitshow of a weekend and the vast research he'd done since that damn leprechaun opened his stupid mouth and let loose that curse, Green had learned that the bad luck came in waves. When one hit, the only safe thing to do was move as little as possible and wait until it passed.

"The weekend was fine," Green lied. "Mostly laid low, slept."

"And avoided using the gas stove or knives?"

Green's shoulders sagged. "Well, yeah, and that."

Bannockburn patted him on the shoulder. "There are all kinds of ways to survive a bit of bad luck, Rookie. You'll figure it out. I'm impressed you decided to waive your rights and accept the hazard pay. Didn't know you had that kind of grit in you."

Green accepted the backhanded compliment and kept his mouth shut, deciding to soak up the praise rather than deflate it by mentioning how, if he'd opted to take leave instead, forfeiting the usual amount of overtime money he pulled in, he'd fall massively behind on all his credit card payments that had amassed while he was on piddly cadet pay.

"I guess you haven't experienced any symptoms?" Green said.

"Nah. Unless you count the suspension."

"Suspension?" Green spat. "For what?"

Bannockburn rolled his neck in large circles and rotated his shoulder to loosen up before another long night. "Oh, you know. Sticking my nose where it didn't belong at the warehouse."

"But you just got a commendation for that."

The corporal stared at him like he was stupid. "Yeah? And?"

"How long will you be suspended for?"

"Officially? Four days."

"Sheesh." Green massaged his temples. "So, we'll be even more short staffed. When does the suspension start?"

Bannockburn laughed. "Oh, it's already going. I'm technically suspended. At this very moment. But because we're so hard-pressed for numbers on this shift, they put out for an overtime officer to fill in. Of course, the shortage isn't limited to our shift. It's a city-wide problem. Dunno if the recruiters are incompetent or hell-bent on the destruction of this city. Anyway, due to various overtime restrictions placed upon us by the great City of Kilhaven and the Kilhaven Police Union, there's only one healthy officer available to work overtime to fill my spot. And you're looking at him." He grinned. "Feel free to call me Officer Bannockburn for the next four days, since that'll technically be my role. Of course, I'll still get compensated time and a half of corporal pay, so, really, you can call me whatever the hell you want, and I won't be upset." He reached down, picked up some of Green's spilled supplies and tossed them into the open trunk. "I have this suspension to thank for being able to afford my daughter's braces."

"You have a daughter?"

"Of course I do. I told you, Green, the Bannockburn seed is strong. No condom can contain the gritty willpower of my sperm."

Picturing Bannockburn as a father was a bit of a stretch for Green's limited imagination, but he supposed it was possible. The man was in his late thirties or early forties. The idea of him having at least one failed marriage under his duty belt wasn't a stretch; in fact, it felt almost natural, like it should have been Green's default.

"I suspect my potency is why Valance keeps holding out," Corporal added.

Green blinked rapidly. "Sir?"

"Well, you know, she plays hard to get. I thought acting like we were lovers would work to ease her into the idea, but nope." He waved it off. "Eh, it'll happen eventually. It worked for you with Brooks, right?"

Green's head swiveled as he scanned the parking lot for anyone who might overhear this unprofessional and unnecessary conversation. Harmon was the nearest to them, and he had his earbuds in and bobbed his head as he threw the last of his gear into his trunk and slammed it shut.

"No," said Green finally, "and I didn't try to make it work."

Bannockburn chuckled. "You're a shit liar, Green. Doesn't matter. Once Brooks and Valance come back, we'll have more important things to focus on than getting laid, I'm sure."

"Like?"

Bannockburn cocked his head to the side. "Valance isn't one to take a break from work, even if she's got some little limp dick's curse hanging over her. Don't take this the wrong way, but if *you* can push through it, so can she ... on one leg, blindfolded, hands tied behind her back. Besides, her whole life has been bad luck, so what's a little more?"

While the comparison didn't feel fantastic, Green knew Bannockburn had a solid point. "Maybe she just needs a vacation. Didn't Montoya say it'd been a decade since she last had one?"

"Ha! Valance wouldn't know what to do with herself on vacation. No, whatever idiot up the chain granted her that leave—and I can tell you it wasn't Montoya; he knows better —rather than finding a way to force her to come into work *really* screwed the pooch. Valance is still working; I guarantee you that. She just has more hours to do it now and without Kilhaven PD breathing down her neck."

Green leaned forward, careful not to strain the seat of his

pants in case the wave of bad luck hadn't yet passed. "So, what do you— God dammit!"

Without missing a beat, Bannockburn reached into his back pocket and pulled out a disinfectant wipe, handing it over to Green, who used it to clean the fresh bird shit off his nose. After thoroughly spitting out the bits that dripped down onto his lips, he picked up the conversation again. "What do you think she's doing exactly?"

"You missed a spot." Corporal pointed to his chin. "And Dracula only knows what she's up to. Since the department *still* won't accept that the Irish weren't the beginning and end of the sprinkles issue, she's probably fed up and off doing some commando vigilante shit. And I promise you one thing, Green: when she gets back, she's going to be on fire, and you and I and probably Brooks, too, are going to be engulfed in it, whether we like it or not." He bent over and scooped up the rest of Green's spilled equipment for him. "I tell you what, Rookie. You think you have bad luck because of the curse? Valance is like a whole fog of bad luck all by herself. A sexy, hard-to-get fog that not even my light can penetrate." He groaned softly, staring at nothing in particular before snapping out of his fantasy and looking Green up and down. "Welp. Good luck out there. You're gonna need it."

As he walked away, Green inhaled deeply, trying to sense if the wave was gone. His intuition told him it was, and when he bent over to grab his bag, the seams of his pants held. He let out the breath he'd been holding.

Sliding into the driver's seat, he closed his eyes to focus his mind. He could do this. He could make it through the waves of bad luck and do so with, dare he say it, style and grace. It was just a matter of practice. All he had to do was regularly tune into his body like he was right then, and sense when the next wave of bad luck was on its way. No big deal. He had this.

He started the engine.

Immediately the siren blared, causing him and those remaining in the parking lot to jump.

Lawrence glared at him and shook his head.

Damn.

He killed the engine and opened the car door. His pant leg snagged on the corner as he stepped out, and he felt the cloth give as it tore.

Fuck.

But he managed not to trip and righted himself quickly. "Sorry!" he hollered at Lawrence, who shook his head again and climbed into his SUV.

Maybe the car was defective. He'd go sign out a new one from the depot. He closed the car door and took a step back toward the substation.

Something warm and gooey landed on his forehead and dripped down his nose.

Shit.

He opened the door again reaching across for the center console where he kept his disinfectant wipes.

And that's when he heard the familiar ripping sound and felt the cool night breeze caressing the fabric of his briefs.

Sonuvabitch!

END OF BOOK 2

Turn the page for more from Kilhaven...

**Don't stop now.
Grab the next Kilhaven Police.**

Killer clown sightings.
Green catches the chief's eye.
Valance continues to be a scary bitch.
You will love this shit.

www.books2read.com/kilhaven3

HEX TRAFFICKING

Two Kilhaven Police officers pulled over a commercial semi-truck traveling north on FM 293 at 1:30pm last Monday after it was seen careening between lanes. Officers suspected the driver, Margery Roan Huffman, human, 49, of distracted driving and pulled her over to issue her a verbal warning. However, during the verbal interaction, officers report that she began acting erratic and agitated, and they asked her to step out of the truck so the cargo could be searched. At first glance the enclose cargo space appeared empty, but upon closer examination, a false bottom was found. In it were 7,000 hex bags, some of which had broken open during transit.

Huffman was arrested and Stubborn Hauntings Unit agents were called to the scene immediately. Huffman claims she was herself under a hex that could only be lifted if she completed the shipment, but she refused to provide further information as to who might have hexed her or why. She faces up to twenty years in prison for hex trafficking and two counts of hexing a law enforcement officer. Both officers suffered severe boils and unwanted erections as a result of the broken hex bags and are still undergoing testing and treatment by licensed witchcraft professionals.

———

Want wild weekly dispatches from Kilhaven sent straight to your inbox? Get a year's subscription to hilarious highway pursuits and bonkers drugs busts when you subscribe to the Kilhaven Police Blotter.

Sign up:
www.ffs.media/kpb

BROCK BLOODWORTH is a private person. He wishes to remain "off the grid" as much as possible. You will not find him on social media, so don't waste your time. If you wish to reach him, consider contacting H. Claire Taylor instead. She's much friendlier.

H. CLAIRE TAYLOR is the author of the Jessica Christ series and deserves a morsel of credit for co-writing the Kilhaven Police series and putting up with Brock's shit. You can learn more about her and her comedy projects at www.hclairetaylor.com.

Find more by Brock and Claire:
www.ffs.media
contact@ffs.media

facebook.com/authorhclairetaylor

twitter.com/claireorwhatevs

bookbub.com/authors/hclairetaylor

goodreads.com/hclairetaylor

amazon.com/author/hclairetaylor